S0-BEB-517

HOCKEY

DREAMS

BY

Gil Conrad

www.scobre.com

Hockey Dreams. COPYRIGHT 2006
by Scott Blumenthal and Brett Hodus
All rights reserved. Printed in Canada.
No part of this book may be used or
reproduced in any manner whatsoever
without written permission, except in the
case of brief quotations embodied in
critical articles and reviews.
For information about Scobre...

Scobre Press Corporation
2255 Calle Clara
La Jolla, CA 92307

First Scobre edition published 2005.

Edited by Anne Greenawalt
Illustrated by Gail Piazza
Cover Design by Michael Lynch

ISBN 1-933423-25-0

www.scobre.com

TOUCHDOWN EDITION

CHAPTER ONE

NEW SKATES

Sitting on a stool in the locker room at the Elk Arena in Saint Paul, Minnesota, on the night of my first NHL game, I can finally sit back and reflect about how in the world I got here. Standing at five feet six inches tall and weighing just over 160 pounds, I am the smallest player on the Minnesota Elk, and probably one of the smallest in the league. That won't stop me, though. I am determined to be a great NHL player.

The locker room is exactly the way I've imagined it all my life. Although I am a player now, I am still not completely comfortable in this room. It will probably be a while before I am. A few of the veteran guys on the team are looking me over as they prepare for the beginning of another long NHL season. I recognize most of them, because I have been cheering for this team since I was in diapers. Being in the same room with professional hockey players, though, is much different than watching them on TV.

My eyes dart around the room—guys are putting tape on their sticks, others listen to music, and two or three players seem to be asleep. I nod my head in the direction of a giant rookie defenseman. I remember Doug Callan from college. His eyes are the only pair in the room as wide as mine. Doug had knocked me around a few times during an NCAA tournament game we played last year. He smiles over at me, raising his eyebrows high, so that they are nearly merging with his hairline. This look seems to ask: can you believe where you and I are standing right now?

After taking a deep breath, I pull on my white, green, and red game jersey and a chill runs down my spine. I'm actually here, in the locker room of the Minnesota Elk. All the people who told me I was too short, too skinny—they were all wrong. I just celebrated my twenty-second birthday, and in about twenty minutes, my lifelong dream will come true.

I grab a pair of brand-new size eight skates from my enormous locker. The blade at the bottom of the skate is shiny and newly sharpened. My number, 44, is stitched into the back of them. As I run my finger along the skate, I close my eyes, remembering my first pair.

I was just seven years old when my parents bought them for me. They were black and white with light blue laces. I still have them today. When I opened the box they were wrapped in, I recognized them right away. They had been in the display window at the Hockey Warehouse, a sporting goods store in the Brookville Mall, for a few months. Every time we passed by the store, I would ask Mom to *please* buy them for me, but she'd always tell me the same thing: "Hockey is too dangerous for such a little boy, Wayne."

Each day after school let out, I would come home carrying a stack of sign-up sheets for Midget Hockey—the youngest age group for organized youth hockey in Robbinsdale. Second grade was the first year a kid could sign up. After just three weeks into the new school year, hockey flyers littered our house. I put them up with hockey magnets on the refrigerator, under Mom's pillow, in Dad's briefcase, and I even used them as place mats when Mom made me set the table.

With constant pressure, and Mom realizing that other kids my age were starting to play hockey, she finally caved in. Inside the box of skates was a signed parental consent form—I was going to play hockey.

Lacing my new skates up on the living room floor was no easy task. Dad warned me about how important it is to lace skates properly. I knew that if I missed a loop or twisted the laces, the skates wouldn't respond properly and I could end up getting hurt. This knowledge forced me to really take my time. As I pulled the laces through the tiny holes in the black leather, my dad told me, "Hockey starts with your feet, Wayne. Great hockey players have great balance—great feet."

Whenever Dad started a sentence with the word hockey I always paid complete attention. And in the Miller house, lots of sentences started with that word. Jack Miller, my father, lived and breathed hockey. And from the time I was a baby, he breathed it into me. "Hockey's a game that requires talent—that's true. But the best players aren't always the most talented. They're the guys with the biggest hearts. Talent isn't enough. Size isn't enough. A great hockey player never quits, Wayne. He's always looking for a way to get involved, and get to the puck."

Putting on my new footwear was awkward and difficult. The skates were tight and very uncomfortable. They were nearly impossible to slip into. Of course, it didn't help that I tricked my mother into getting me skates one size smaller than my shoe size. After all, I figured, that was the way the pros did it. Even when I was seven, the NHL was a really big deal to me. So, a few days earlier, when Mom asked me to check the tongue of my gym shoes for my size, I told her they were a six, even though I knew they were a seven.

Because they were hockey skates, as opposed to figure skates, they were sturdy and heavy, even a bit clunky. The sharp metal blade at the base of the skate was supported by thick plastic. The tongue was huge, and the high ankle support wasn't something I was used to. To be honest, wearing them felt something like wearing cement blocks. Plus, the leather was hard and cut into my ankle.

"Do they fit?" Mom asked, unconvinced.

I hid the pained expression on my face. "Yeah, I think so."

As I struggled to wiggle my toes for Mom, all I could think of was getting on the ice and moving with the grace and speed of Wayne Gretzky—the man who is widely known as the greatest hockey player of all time. I had been following "The Great One's" career my entire life. My parents, who grew up in Edmonton, Alberta, in Canada, had been Gretzky fans since before I was born. They even had a hockey puck displayed on the mantle in the living room that he had autographed. When my parents found out they were having a boy, they easily picked out a name for me—Wayne. Needless to say, I had a lot to live up to.

Once the skates were securely on my feet, I tried to stand.

I was unsuccessful. The blades dug into our grey-brown carpet, causing me to lose my balance and fall flat on my back. I smacked my head on the side of the couch but stood up again right away. Although I was a bit frustrated, I was also excited. Dad had promised to take me skating at Medicine Lake in the morning, but this simply couldn't wait. I begged them to let me go down to Mickey's Ice Arena with Dad, who was going to meet some friends for a pick-up game. I told them I could watch him play, and when he was finished, he could let me come out onto the ice. It didn't even matter if it was only for a few minutes. I just *had* to try out my skates on the ice—tonight.

It didn't take much pleading for them to let me go. Mom wanted to come, too, so she wouldn't miss the experience of watching me skate for the first time. When we hopped in the car, my legs felt almost completely numb from the tightness of the skates around my ankles. Still, I couldn't stop smiling.

We made our way through the winding streets of Robbinsdale, the Minnesota town where I was born. Hockey was a big part of life in our town. The town was pretty small, with a few restaurants, an ice cream shop, and a movie theatre, where all the high school kids hung out. We also had two hockey stores and three ice rinks, not including the ones at the middle school and the high school. Nobody in town ever missed a Minnesota Elk game. The NHL franchise is located in the city of Saint Paul, just a few minutes away. Although we rooted hard for our football and baseball teams, when it came to hockey, we were fanatics—we went absolutely nuts for the Elk.

The drive from our house to the ice rink was only about ten minutes, but the anticipation of finally getting on the ice made it feel more like thirty. When we pulled up and I saw the sign that read Mickey's Ice Arena, my heart jumped. Aside from a few Elk playoff games I had watched on television, my most vivid hockey memories are from the games I witnessed there live. The hockey played there was serious, rough at times, and highly competitive. Aside from pick-up games, Dad also played in the Men's Intramural League every Wednesday night. So Mom and I were always hanging out at Mickey's.

I'd been on the ice a bunch of times in my life, but never in a pair of skates. That was because I hadn't owned skates until an hour earlier. For the first time, I was going to step onto the ice and actually skate! I looked over at my mother and she smiled. She shut the car off and said, "Now, Wayne, this is your first time out there, so promise me you'll take it slow." I had a history of being a little too fearless in my life, like the time I rode my bike down an ice-covered hill in Lion's Park with the older boys in my town. I hit a bad bump, flew over my handle bars, and broke my arm. Mom already looked worried.

"I promise," I said with my smile spreading from ear to ear.

My mother and I sat in folding chairs just on the outskirts of center ice. My dad waved at us as he grabbed his hockey stick and jumped onto the ice. Although I loved watching him play, tonight was different. Tonight was going to be my turn. I could hardly stay seated as I watched Dad and the other men skate with speed around the rink, and hit the puck with such force that it became invisible. At one point, a man much smaller than my dad came from behind him and smashed him against the wall. Dad went down, but got up quickly and smiled at me. I didn't smile back. I was too busy daydreaming about being on the ice, starting Midget Hockey, and eventually playing alongside Dad.

At six feet four inches tall, Dad had been a powerful forward for his high school team. He set a Canadian scoring record during his junior season. There's a really cool plaque up at his high school with his name on it. Dad says that if things would have gone differently, he would have made it to the NHL. But when he broke his leg badly during the last game of his senior season, his NHL dreams fell apart. Dad was in a wheelchair for a year. Eventually, he was able to walk, and skate again, too. By that time, though, his window of opportunity had closed. Hockey became his hobby, but it was no longer a career option.

These pick-up games were something he did for fun, but that didn't mean he didn't take them seriously. During league games on Wednesday nights, a different side of my father would come out. He was a competitor, a warrior, a tough-as-nails athlete, who, though well past his prime, could still play the game at a high level. I desperately wanted to play like him some day—but even better.

Just when I thought I couldn't wait another second to get on the ice, the game paused for a moment. Dad said something to one of his teammates and skated over to us at full speed. His legs pumped as he pushed off the ice with smooth and powerful movements. When he was about five feet from us, he stopped short, pushing the side of his skate into the ice, and spraying a thin mist of snow right at my face. As I wiped the snow from my eyes, Dad grabbed me, lifting me in the air and over the boards.

He planted me on the ice and I held his shirt for balance. He then called over to the man who had just crushed him a moment earlier. "Phil, let's call it a night, okay? Little Wayne got a pair of skates. He's gonna try 'em out for a bit."

Even though I was just seven years old, I'll never forget standing there on the ice. I'll never forget how strange the slippery surface felt beneath the blades. In that moment, I couldn't understand how Dad moved the way he did. I couldn't imagine ever being in control like that on the ice. It was too slippery, the blade was too thin, my ankles kept rolling, and I kept falling to the ground. And I hadn't even tried to skate yet! It didn't make sense. How was it possible to have control of my body when all of my weight was concentrated on a blade no thicker than the point of a pencil? Standing on ice in sneakers was hard enough! How was I ever going to be good at this?

I never had the chance to answer those questions, because in the midst of my doubts, Dad grabbed me by the hand and started to skate. "Hang on tight!" he yelled.

He took off, pumping his legs and moving his arms quickly, up and down across the sides of his body. For a forty-year-old man, he was lightning fast. We started at center ice and made our way toward the far goal first. "Do you want me to slow down, Wayne? If you're scared, I can."

Although every ounce of logic in my brain was telling me to say yes, my sense of adventure took over. "No! This is great! Go faster!"

"Faster? Okay—here we go." Then he *really* took off. We skated from goal to goal at full speed. Tiny pieces of ice shot up and hit my face as Dad's skates cut across the ice. My brown hair blew back from my face in the wind. I was really skating! Well, my father was skating—I was coasting. Still, it felt amazing! Holding tight to Dad's jacket, the thin blades on the base of my new skates kissed the ground below them, barely making contact with the ice.

"Yeah!" I yelled at the top of my lungs. "I'm flying!"

Mom watched us closely from outside the rink, occasionally yelling "slow down" or "Jack, he's a little boy!" Dad skated with me holding onto him tightly for awhile. Occasionally I slipped, but I was scooped up by my father, who never stopped moving or lost his balance—even for a second.

After about ten minutes, we reached the far goal and Dad stopped. Sweat beads had formed on his head and he was breathing heavy. With his hands resting on his knees, he told me to try skating on my own for a bit. So I did. Even though I never got more than a few feet without falling, I was hooked on the feeling. I listened carefully to Dad's advice, bending my knees and pushing off the ice, using the back of my blades as an anchor.

"Stay right here," Dad said, skating back to the far goal, where two hockey sticks lay on top of the empty net. He grabbed them both and made his way back toward me near center ice. Then he handed me a stick that was much too big for me. He dropped a puck onto the ice. I slowly skated forward until I was about twenty feet from the goal, staring at it. "Take a shot, Wayne. Shift your weight back with the stick and then forward when you hit the puck. But stay low. And make sure to hit the ice before the puck. Oh, and snap your wrist on the follow-through, too." I looked back at him with one eyebrow raised in confusion. "Just hit it," he said.

Easy for you to say, I thought. I zeroed in on the goal as I tried to stay balanced. Then I imagined myself being a professional with an open shot. I bent my knees the way I'd seen Wayne Gretzky do a thousand times before as he unleashed a slap shot. I gripped the giant stick with two hands, one near the top and one closer to the middle. Then I reached back and swung at the puck with all of my might, hitting the ground about six inches behind it.

Because the stick was so large, I lost my balance and fell backwards. The follow through of my stick still connected with the puck. Even though I was falling, I made sure to snap my wrist. Dropping my stick to the ground, I hit the ice with a loud thud and banged my head on the hard surface.

I lay there on the ice with a big bump on my head. Mom ran out to see if I was okay. She yelled at my father as he skated over to me. She sat down in front of me, blocking my view of the goal as she rubbed my head. My eyes welled up with tears, but I fought hard against crying. "Are you okay, sweetheart?" Mom said, kissing the top of my head.

"You alright, champ?" Dad followed. "Keep your balance next time. I liked the way you snapped your wrist, but you have to focus on the—"

"Jack!" Mom interjected. "The boy just hit his head. Give him a second." Dad never stopped coaching me.

A single tear streamed down my cheek. As Dad lifted me back up to my feet, I looked over his shoulder through the tears. There, sitting in the corner of the goal, was the puck. I'd made it.

A huge smile swept across my face.

CHAPTER TWO

LITTLE WAYNE

The Minnesota Elk locker room is awesome. The ceiling is high, and the walls are adorned with framed pictures of NHL legends. The floor is covered with a lush green carpet that has an enormous Elk logo in the center of it. Several black leather couches face flat screen televisions that hang from all four corners of the room. Our lockers are solid oak, flanked by vending machines that don't ask for quarters. This place is like an amusement park for hockey-junkies.

We're playing the Chicago Firestorm tonight and Coach Lewis comes into the room to go over some last-minute strategy. I listen extra closely as he talks about our forwards pushing up on offense without losing sight of our defensive responsibilities. He is jotting a few things down on a dry-erase board in front of us. I take a mental note of every word this man says.

Like my father, I am a forward. A few months earlier, I was the seventeenth pick for the Minnesota Elk in the second

round of this year's NHL draft. In terms of the Elk's front of-
fice expectations, I don't think there are too many. I know the
odds are against me. Many guys drafted in the middle of the
second round end up playing in obscure European leagues,
coaching, or waiting tables for a living.

Despite all of that, I believe I am going to make an
impact in this league, and it's going to start tonight. Coach
leaves the room and I continue to put on my gear. I drop my left
shin pad onto the floor. One of the older guys, veteran forward
John Simpson, takes his stick and slaps my shin pad over to
Alexi Kornikov. The large Russian laughs, and shoots my pad
back to John.

I stand up, not willing to let the older guys mess with
my stuff. Being bullied is something I remember too well from
my childhood. I know that I have to put an end to this right
here and now or I will be dealing with it all season long. As I
make eye contact with one of my new teammates, I remember
a time in my life when I was in a similar situation.

One of the biggest changes an elementary school kid goes
through when entering middle school is dealing with a locker. Well,
on my first day at Robbinsdale Middle School, my locker got
stuck—and no matter how hard I pulled, it simply wouldn't open.
This meant that I couldn't get my science book out. This also meant
that I was about to be late to my second period class with the
infamous Mr. Weathers.

As I stood in front of my locker, the late bell rang loudly.
The hallways, which were crowded a moment earlier, quickly emp-
tied out. About ten seconds later, I was all alone. Sweat began to

form beneath my armpits and on my forehead. *I couldn't show up late and unprepared for my first day of class.* I pulled at the locker again, this time with all of my might. It wouldn't budge, though. I couldn't get a good enough grip on the door.

Just then, a light went on in my head. I had an idea. I frantically took the shoelace off of my right shoe and tied it around the handle of my locker. With my right shoe flopping around loosely on my foot, I pulled and tugged on the lace with all of my might. I used every ounce of strength I had in my body. Finally, it gave. The locker door broke open with a loud crash and I fell back across the hallway, holding a shoelace that was now attached to the dangling metal door of my locker. I had torn it clear off the wall.

Completely rattled by my broken locker, I dropped the metal door into a nearby garbage can, with my shoelace still attached to it. Then I pulled my right shoe off of my foot and tucked it under my arm. What had started as a small problem, was now a total disaster. Trying to control the damage, I grabbed my book and sprinted to class. In my hurriedness, though, I didn't realize that science wasn't the only yellow textbook in my locker. My English book was yellow as well.

When I walked into class, Mr. Weathers, along with everyone else in the class was staring at me. I must have looked ridiculous. I was carrying my right shoe under my arm, and I was sweating from head to toe.

A few minutes later, I had caught my breath and was settling into class. In my head, I formulated a plan: after class, I would go to the nurse's office and borrow a shoelace. Next, I would go to the principal's office, and request a new locker. Everything would work out.

In the middle of these thoughts, we started our discussion on the layers of the earth's crust. Unfortunately, I was the first person called on to read. I quickly confessed that I had left my science book in my locker and accidentally brought my English book. "They're both yellow," I said.

Mr. Weathers didn't seem to care. He stared at me as though I was a criminal.

"I can read a page from this book for you," I offered, but my suggestion didn't have the desired effect. Instead of letting me off the hook, Mr. Weathers pointed me out to the entire class, saying that I appeared to be a "disorganized little fella," and, that succeeding in his class without the proper books was impossible. Everyone was staring at me.

The "disorganized" part didn't bother me half as much as the "little fella." I was definitely small—probably the smallest boy in school—but that didn't mean I needed to be reminded about it all the time. It was bad enough that almost everyone I knew called me "Little Wayne"—both because I was little *and* because Wayne Gretzky, whom I was named after, was big in name and stature. I hated that nickname.

I made it through the next few periods without incident. I got a new shoelace, and a new locker, too. When I headed to the cafeteria for lunch, my day was starting to improve. I was going to get through this.

In the pocket of my sweatshirt, I gripped my lucky hockey puck tightly. It was the same puck I had scored with when I was just seven years old playing with my Dad at Mickey's Ice Arena. I pretty much carried it with me wherever I went. I squeezed it, rubbed the palm of my hand on it, and spun it in circles on my lap during class. I loved that puck, and I was sure that it brought me good luck. On this day, though, it did just the opposite.

The school cafeteria was shaped like a giant square with about fifteen circular tables spread throughout. Right when I got there, I looked around frantically for a table and a place to sit. As far as I was concerned, sitting alone at lunch was as bad as it got for a middle school kid. When I saw my best friend, Ricky Vang, sitting at a table with an empty seat next to him, I sighed with relief and waved to him. Quick Rick, as we called him on our elementary school hockey team, had already gotten his lunch and was halfway through it. The funny thing was, Ricky wasn't quick at all on the ice. He was actually pretty slow and goofy. He did everything else fast, though, like getting dressed, lacing his skates, or eating a burger. It was a perfect nickname for him.

I walked over to the lunch line and grabbed a plastic tray. I picked up a carton of milk and scooped a helping of spaghetti and meatballs onto my plate. From the corner of my eye, I noticed Darius Gray and a group of familiar-looking guys walking toward the line. Darius, Javier Cervantes, Mike DePeppo, and Brock Landon were the most talented hockey players in school. I recognized them from pick-up games I had seen them play. These guys were all eighth graders. They were all big and bad.

Darius Gray was the star of the middle school hockey team. He was also well-known for being a dirty player, as mean as he was popular. He was a full foot taller than me, with a broad chest, large biceps, and a hairy chin. As I stood in line, I didn't even notice that I was staring right at him. Unfortunately, he *did* notice and approached me. "Can I help you with something?" Darius's voice had a harsh tone.

"What?" I asked, totally confused.

"Why . . . are . . . you . . . staring . . . at . . . me . . .?" he asked.

"I . . . I wasn't." My heart raced as I answered.

He took a few more steps toward me and slid in front of me in line, grabbing a tray and piling food onto it. "I'm in a hurry," he said, explaining why he was cutting in front of me.

I didn't respond. I just let him cut. While we waited, he pointed to my Minnesota Elk sweatshirt and asked, "You a hockey fan?"

"Yes," I answered. I have to admit, I was kind of excited that the older hockey star was speaking to me. Maybe he had seen me play. Maybe he was excited about the chance for me to be his teammate—that is, if I made the middle school team. "I play, you know. Last year I started at forward on the—"

"*You* play?" He started laughing at me as if the idea of me playing hockey was the funniest thing he'd ever heard in his life.

"Yeah," I answered, with as much toughness as I could muster. "I'm going out for the team, too. So I'll probably see you next week at tryouts."

He called over to Javier, who was talking to two of the prettiest girls in school—Tanya Willis and April Lemanski. "Javier, come over here and meet this guy. He's hilarious. He thinks he's making the team."

Javier Cervantes, who was fairly tall and quite heavy, came barreling over to us. He looked at me, laughed, and then bumped knuckles with Darius. "I've eaten sandwiches bigger than you, little man. Maybe you could be our mascot. Or better yet, you could be a jockey!" He held his stomach as he laughed loudly at his joke.

That was the second time I had been called little in the course of the day, and it really ticked me off.

At this point, April and Tanya were laughing, and most of the kids in the room were staring at me. I wanted to disappear. Instead, I said the dumbest thing possible: "I may be little, but put me in a pair of skates and I'll knock both of you into the boards so hard you'll be seeing stars."

"What did you just say?" Javier took a big step toward me.

"You heard me. I said I'll knock you out when it counts."

Before I could brace myself for the punch that I was sure would follow my comment, the woman at the cash register addressed me. "That'll be one dollar and seventy cents, please."

With Javier so close to me that I could taste his lunch, and Darius standing directly to his left, I wasn't sure what would happen next. Kids who were sitting in the back row of the cafeteria a moment earlier, were now standing. They all wanted to see the little guy get knocked out by giant Javier. I wondered how I was going to reach my seat without getting killed. I actually thought about making a run for it. I also thought about throwing my tray of spaghetti at Javier, taking a quick swing at Darius, and seeing what happened from there. My final thought was that after today I was probably going to have to change schools.

"A dollar seventy, Hon," the woman behind the register repeated. I realized that I was holding up the entire lunch line.

Javier and Darius just stood there, unsure of their next move. My comments had not only attracted the attention of the students who were eating, but a few teachers as well. The two hockey stars couldn't just beat me up in the middle of the cafeteria. They would get into trouble for that.

"If you don't have the dollar seventy, you need to step out of line."

"Sorry," I said, finally reaching into my pocket and grabbing the two dollars Mom had given me this morning. Just as I was handing the woman my money, something awful happened—my lucky puck dropped out of my pocket. It hit the floor and spun there for a second. As fast as I could, I reached down to grab it. I wasn't fast enough, though. Javier put his massive hand on my shoulder, which stopped me cold. Of course, Darius saw this as a golden opportunity to get to me.

He grabbed the puck and gave me a vicious smile. "You're dead at tryouts, little man. I can't wait." He winked at me as he stuffed the puck into his pocket and calmly walked back to the "cool table."

The woman behind the register handed me back my thirty cents change. My legs felt as heavy as lead as I made my way over to the table where Ricky was sitting in the corner of the cafeteria. As I walked toward him, fifty or sixty sets of eyes were staring at me. This was definitely one of those "did you hear what happened in the cafeteria today" moments. Talk about a bad first impression.

I sat down next to Ricky.

"That went well," he said sarcastically.

"I can't believe I dropped the puck." I said.

"Any reason you just started a fight with the two biggest kids at school?"

I didn't pay any attention to Ricky's comment. Instead, I kept looking over his shoulder at the table Darius and Javier were sitting at. My eyes were locked on my puck. "I want my puck back, Ricky."

"Forget it, Wayne. Your puck is gone."

I stared down into my plate of spaghetti. Then I picked up one of the golf ball sized meatballs and stuffed the entire thing into my mouth. I glared over at Darius Gray —and chewed and chewed and chewed.

Ricky tapped me on the shoulder. "Dude, stop doing that."

I kept chewing.

"Stop doing that! You're killing us. Fighting with the hockey team is one thing, grossing out the girls is another. I have to draw the line somewhere." Ricky stood in front of me so that I was blocked from view. "Don't make me take away that second meatball. I will, Wayne. For your own good I will."

I swallowed the meatball and knew exactly what I had to do next. "I'll be right back. I have to get my puck." With that comment hanging in the air, I stood up and started my walk over to the "cool table." Now my heart was really thumping.

There were seven of them sitting there. Darius, Javier, Brock, and Mike, along with three eighth-grade girls I'd only heard of. Darius stood up when I got close to the table. He took my puck from his pocket and began tossing it up into the air and catching it. He was taunting me.

"Will you please give me my puck back?" I asked nicely.

"Don't be such a jerk, Darius. Just give him his puck back." Jennifer Davis said.

"This is my puck, Jen." Darius answered, flipping the puck up again. "I found it on the floor." He got real close to me, so that my nose was in his chest. "You can't just leave things on the floor like you don't want them, you little dwarf."

"I do want it. You saw me drop it. You know it's mine." By

this time I was pretty sure that Darius wasn't going to *give* me back my lucky puck. I was going to have to take it. With my hand braced against the side of the round table I tried one last time. "Please Darius, just give it back. That puck means a lot to me."

That was when Darius started to yell. "The puck is mine! I guess little guys like you have little brains too. You must be the dumbest kid I've ever met. Get lost!" he said, pushing me backwards.

There are certain moments in life when you realize that you are past the point of no return. This was one of those moments for me. No matter what I did from this point forward, Darius Gray was going to be my enemy. There was nothing I could do to stop that. I decided that if he was going to be my enemy anyway, I might as well get my puck back. So I did the only thing I could think of: I grabbed a handful of spaghetti and meatballs from Jennifer Davis's tray and threw it in Darius's face.

What happened next was predictable. Darius knocked me to the floor with a punch that landed right on the side of my mouth. While I was on the ground, he took the rest of Jennifer's lunch and poured it on my head. He then grabbed Javier's lunch and poured that on my head—then April's lunch, then Mike's, too.

Just as Darius was pouring the rest of Brock's milk on my head, Mr. Weathers came over. He yelled at Darius, then at me, and we both ended up in detention for the next two days. That was the bad news. The good news was that while I was on the ground, and Darius was covering me with spaghetti, meatballs, and milk, he dropped my puck.

I put it back in my pocket before being escorted to the principal's office.

CHAPTER THREE

TRYOUTS

I can feel my blood beginning to boil as my new team-mates continue to slap my shin pads around on the locker room floor. After a minute or so, Alexi Kornikov notices that I am on my feet, staring at him. He can sense my pulse racing. With his stick up in the air, about to smash down on my shin pad, he looks over at me. Our eyes meet and the strange Russian laughs. "Okay, I leave it alone. I can tell that you feisty—I like feisty." He then lifts up my shin pad and gently tosses it to me. "I'm feisty too," he smiles, revealing a mouth with several missing teeth. His smile seems to shout: Welcome to the NHL—the toughest league in professional sports.

"Thanks," I say, sitting back down to put on the rest of my gear. A sense of relief rushes over me. I am not sure, but I may have just made a friend. I finish taping, and bending my stick, to provide just the right amount of curve. I glance into my locker at ten more sticks that look just like this one. They

are all mine. Starting tonight, I will begin to compete against some of the toughest, most athletic men in the world. There will certainly be some broken sticks along the way. I am sure there will be some broken bones as well.

A moment later, a man in a suit pops his head into the locker room. "Five minutes, guys." Hearing this voice makes me nervous, and I am fully aware that my stomach is filled with butterflies. We are about to take the ice.

Twenty-two players make up our team. In hockey, most players on a roster will get into every game. This is extra exciting for us rookies, as we know we will be seeing ice time from day one. Line changes will occur throughout the course of a game, which means that some, or all, of the players on the ice will be replaced by other players, again and again. This rotation happens constantly. But unlike basketball, football, or baseball, play does not stop. Players enter and exit the game during live play. Line changes are fast and must be done at the exact right moment so that the other team is unable to take advantage of empty ice.

So far, I am considered an offensive sub—a player without a definitive role. I am pretty sure that I am not a penalty killer, and I'm definitely not part of the checking line. Being a rookie, I am certainly not on the first or second line either. The pace of play, penalties, injuries, and other variables will dictate my playing time. Coach has assured me and the other rookie, Doug Calan—that we are going to get in there. He just doesn't know for how long or when. This is why I have to be at full attention during the game, because at any moment, my number can be called.

All of my gear is on and I stand up again, stretching my back and my knees. I'm nervous, but filled with confidence at the same time. Following my teammates, I make my way down the long tunnel which leads to the arena. I have been waiting to take this walk my entire life. I am in the middle of the pack, lost in a sea of giant bodies. I take a deep breath as I am finally able to see the bright lights of the arena at the end of the tunnel.

"Here we go," I whisper.

When I got home from school after the spaghetti incident, I ran straight to the laundry room. I'd been forced to sit through half of my day in clothes drenched in Monday's lunch. By the time I got home, I was sticky and gross—not to mention the smell. I kept looking over my shoulder as I undressed to make sure my parents didn't walk in and notice my clothes. There was no way I would be able to explain what happened to them. I dropped my jeans and sweatshirt into the washing machine, throwing in a capful of laundry detergent the way I had seen Mom do. I made sure to remove my puck from the pocket of my sweatshirt.

I jumped into the shower, scrubbed tomato sauce out of my hair, and picked a few tiny pieces of meatballs out from the inside of my ears. Then I walked into my bedroom and threw on a pair of sweatpants and a t-shirt. Grabbing a pencil from my backpack, I stood with my back to the wall next to my bedroom doorway. I had been making marks on that wall since my first day of kindergarten. I leaned my head back, and made a horizontal line with a pencil. I was pretty sure that I had grown a little bit. After all, it had been a full year since I had made my last mark.

This can't be right, I thought. The line I drew was directly on top of last year's line. I hadn't even grown a quarter inch! I stood at four feet four inches tall—again.

That night, I sat down on my computer and looked up different ways people could help themselves grow. I found a bunch of methods that were supposed to make you tall. There were all these stretches I could do, and a bunch of herbs I could eat. One website even suggested that I sleep standing up. It all sounded pretty stupid to me. I didn't plan on wasting my time with any of that stuff. Like Mom always said, I just had to be patient.

The next week at school was okay. Aside from the fact that the two toughest kids in school wanted to kill me, the incident in the cafeteria didn't turn out to be all that terrible. Actually, lots of kids, especially some of the smaller guys at school, came up to me in the hallway to slap my hand and tell me how cool it was that I stood up to Darius Gray. A few girls even talked to me, and that *never* happened. My big mouth may have actually paid off for once.

Ricky, on the other hand, was scared stiff. He and Darius had lockers that were pretty close together. This meant that every time they saw each other, which was about ten times a day, Darius would harass my best friend. He would push Ricky into his locker and tell him that he and I were dead at hockey tryouts. I felt terrible for Ricky. It was my fault. I had dragged him into this. It didn't matter that I hadn't meant to.

By Friday, Ricky was walking around school with a limp. He told me that he had injured his ankle helping his Dad clean out their garage. I didn't buy that story for a second. I knew he was faking it, and wasn't surprised when he told me he wasn't going to try out for the hockey team. I tried to convince him that Darius was just talking, and that nothing would actually come of it, but he wouldn't listen. Honestly, I wasn't sure that I even believed myself.

I wasn't scared of taking a few hard hits from Darius at the tryouts. I just hoped that our feud wouldn't affect my chances of making the team. I thought I had a decent chance. After all, I had started at forward last season for the Lions and led the team in goals. That was elementary school, though, and the competition this year was going to be much tougher. That wasn't going to stop me from trying out, though. And neither was Darius Gray.

Tryouts started on Monday afternoon. About forty kids showed up to earn one of eighteen spots on the team. There were nine returning eighth graders and one returning seventh grader. Assuming that all ten of them would make the team, eight spots remained open for thirty of us. We had one day to show our skills off to Coach Nielson, a large, intimidating man who never stopped blowing his whistle.

I had known Coach Nielson for most of my life. He'd played hockey with my father at Mickey's. He was a right defenseman, and Dad used to say that he was just about the toughest guy he'd ever played with. Coach also had a strange habit that was difficult to get used to. For some reason, he tended to shout the last word of every sentence he spoke. For example: "Okay, guys. Line up here at center ICE!" None of us were sure why he did it, but it took all of our self control not to break out laughing when he did. Still, when he spoke, we listened.

At the beginning of tryouts, the guys lined up at center ice right away. I stood on the tips of my skates, extending my neck to make it look like I was an inch or two taller. Sam Bernard was the only guy I was even close to in terms of height. So I made sure to stand right next to him. Coach skated up and down the ice, staring at each one of us. He gave me a nod with his head, acknowledging that he remembered me from all the games I'd watched him play over the years. I was glad he remembered, but I knew that wasn't going to get me on the team. The town of Robbinsdale took hockey way too seriously for Coach Nielson to play favorites. If he put someone on the team for the wrong reasons, he'd be replaced, and fast.

The format for the tryout was simple: Coach divided us into teams of six players, two teams played each other for about seven minutes, and then we rotated. By the end of the one-day, five-hour tryout, we had all played a lot of hockey. My team was made up of myself, Jack Nix, who was last year's starting goalie, two eighth graders who I'd never seen before, and Brock—one of the top forwards on the team. As luck would have it, we were playing against Darius's team in the first game.

While we were doing the mandatory pre-game stretching routine, I noticed Darius, Javier, Mike, and Brock whispering to each other near center ice. They were looking directly at me while they stretched. There was some pointing and laughing going on, too. Then Darius punched his hand hard. I flinched when I heard the popping sound all the way from the other end of the ice. I tried not to look scared, but I was.

Coach Nielson dropped the puck for the first game about ten minutes later. I was playing right wing, which lined me up directly opposite Darius. The moment the puck was dropped, he came after me. He underestimated my speed, though, and I eluded him, breaking toward the goal. Our center noticed my run and smacked a perfect pass that hit my stick in stride. I flew up the ice, knowing that nobody would be able to catch me. Before the defense closed in, I took a shot on goal. The puck hit the right post and the pinging sound echoed throughout the building. I had just missed.

Their right defenseman controlled the puck off of the deflection and skated up the right side. I recovered, drifting back toward center ice. Brock was playing on the left wing and he managed to steal the puck back. When I saw him with the puck, I flew down the center of the ice and made another run at goal. He saw me and made his pass. It was behind me, however, and when I turned my body to get it, Darius flew in and crushed me with a body check. He led with his shoulder and I fell to the ground. He took off down the ice on a fast break, finishing with a goal.

I stood back up and took a deep breath. Brock was laughing and I wondered if he and Darius had set me up for that hit. "Something funny, Brock?" I asked, loud enough for Coach to hear.

"Be quiet and play hockey! Both of you," he yelled. That was that. Now I knew for sure that these guys were going to be teaming up on me—even Brock, who was supposed to be my teammate.

All I could do to stop them was play my heart out. And I did. A few minutes later, I made another nice run at the goal and took a slap shot that was barely saved. So far, in terms of offense on our team, I was it. Brock was a step too slow and completely intimidated by Darius.

Darius followed me all over the ice, punishing me with one check after another. He must have knocked me down ten times during that seven minute game. There wasn't much I could do about it either. He was two years older than me, strong, athletic, and fast.

Plus, he was mean.

"Thirty seconds, guys," Coach said.

Darius took a shot, and our goalie made a kick save. He passed it up the right boards and I reached my stick out and got it. I took off with one man between me and the goalie. The lone defender started to skate at me, trying to cut off my angle to the goal. He looked like he was gearing up to deliver me a body check—which seemed to be the most popular thing to do on this day. I put my shoulder down and pumped my legs.

As I got closer to him, I stopped short, spinning around so that he skated right past me. It was my best move of the game. When I looked up, it was just me and the goalie. Quickly, I reached back, shifting all of my weight onto my back foot. I had a clear shot on goal.

From nowhere, though, Darius came flying in. I never even saw him. While in my backswing, he laid into me. It was a clean hit that knocked me to the ice with tremendous force. I never got the chance to hit the puck. I lay on the floor, and had to be helped off the ice.

"You alright, Miller?" Coach Nielson asked me.

I tried hard to speak, but Darius had knocked the wind out of me. I nodded my head. "I'm good, Coach." I said, trying not to sound like I was gasping for air.

"Next two groups!" Coach blew his whistle and twelve more guys skated onto the ice.

I sat on the bench drinking from a water bottle. My head hurt, my chest hurt, and my legs hurt. I could feel Coach Nielson's eyes on me. That last hit probably looked terrible and I knew that Coach was worried about me. So I pretended to laugh at something, like I was feeling no pain. The last thing I wanted was for Coach to think I was an injury risk.

A moment later, Darius walked up behind me. He leaned in close and said, "You mess with the bull and you get the horns, little man. There's plenty more where that came from."

Refusing to back down, I said. "Bring it."

And bring it he did. So did Javier, and Mike, and the rest of Darius's friends. For the next few hours, I was a marked man. It seemed like every time I touched the puck I ended up getting flattened. Sure, I scored a goal or two, handled the puck well, played good defense, and proved myself to be the fastest player on the ice. But I was getting knocked around like a rag doll.

During the last game of the day, Coach had seen enough. Javier Cervantes, who outweighed me by close to 100 pounds, knocked me into the boards so hard that we had to replace one of the pieces of plastic. I slumped to the ground slowly before rising to my feet. Coach Nielson blew his whistle again, stopping play. He skated over to me, yelling. "You've got to protect yourself, Miller! Skate with your head up, or you'll get killed out here."

"Yes, Coach," I said.

"Take a seat and catch your breath," Coach said, while skating toward center ice.

I pumped my legs until I reached center ice. Before the puck dropped I said, "I'm okay, Coach. I can stay in."

"I said take a seat, Miller! Nick, get in for Miller."

Totally frustrated, I skated over to the bench and dropped my stick. The tryouts ended a few minutes later.

I kept to myself in the locker room, showering quickly and getting dressed before everybody else. I was back out on the ice in fifteen minutes. One by one, the guys also made their way out. We were all waiting for Coach to exit his small office located just behind the locker room. Darius and his friends stood in a circle, apart from everyone else. They joked and laughed with each other while the rest of us fidgeted nervously. Finally, Coach Nielson vacated his office and joined us on the ice.

I knew that I'd had a pretty good tryout. But I also knew that Coach was looking more and more nervous every time I was knocked to the ice. "Guys, this is the hardest part of being a coach. I really wish I could keep all of you, but I can't." He skated over to the group and began handing out single sheets of paper to us. "I'm handing you a list of this year's team. If your name is on the list, meet here tomorrow at four for practice. If not, thanks for coming out."

When Coach Nielson handed me the list he didn't look me in the eyes. I knew right then that I had been cut. I checked the list anyway, but the name Miller was nowhere to be found. I hung my head, devastated.

Darius skated past me on his way out, "Better luck next year, little man." He and Javier laughed as they left the building. I clenched the muscles in my face to hold back the tears that wanted to pour out.

When everyone was gone I sat there on the bench alone. I knew that my Mom was probably waiting for me out front, but I just couldn't move. Coach Nielson sat down beside me. "You play just like your Dad, Wayne."

"Thank you," I said respectfully, but avoiding eye contact. "My father never got cut from a team, though, sir."

"Don't get down. You're a real talented kid, maybe the

most talented player out there. And you've got heart." He paused, "But Wayne—"

I cut him off, "I'm too small, right? Talent isn't enough."

"I'm afraid you're going to get hurt, son. You're only twelve and these guys are older than you—and much bigger. Hockey's a rough sport. You saw it today. You were getting killed out there."

"You took me out, Coach. I never took myself out. I scored twice and I'm the fastest guy out there. I can help this team win. I'm not scared of taking a hit."

Coach looked me right in the eyes when he said: "That's what I'm afraid of. Your Dad played the same way and look what happened to him. And he was big, Wayne. I just—I can't put you out there right now."

I swallowed hard and got to my feet. "I guess I understand," I said. Then I shook his hand and left the building.

Darius and his idiot friends had ruined my chances. My big mouth had cost me more than the black and blue marks I was going to have in the morning—it cost me a spot on the team.

CHAPTER FOUR

THE EQUIPMENT MANAGER

As we make our way into the arena, I squint, trying to give my eyes a chance to adjust to the blinding lights. As a team, we begin to skate around in a circle. The fans are loud and excited for the season's opening game. The feeling in the air is unlike any that I have experienced. It's amazing.

Most of the players try to ignore the boisterous crowd, attempting to focus on their pre-game rituals. John Simpson, a three-time All-Star, skates directly in front of me. I can remember watching him on television in my living room as a child. He moves his head from side to side as he skates, speeding up and then slowing down. Having been here before, he seems completely calm.

I can't help but stare at the people who fill nearly every seat in the enormous arena. My head is on a swivel, taking in a professional hockey game—from the ice. I begin looking for my parents, just like I did during my first game in youth hockey.

After a minute or two, I find them. They're both dressed from head to toe in Minnesota Elk gear. They are parked about ten rows up near center ice and look as excited as I am. Dad gives me an intense fist pump when he notices me looking at him. Mom snaps a picture. I don't dare wave at them.

After skating a few laps around the ice, we spread out for some passing drills and to take some shots on goal. At this point, our opponents have entered the arena and a few boos can be heard echoing off the rafters above my head. The Chicago Firestorm skate around and begin their warm-ups as well. Being a huge hockey fan, it's hard not to look at some of my teammates and opponents in awe—the way I did when I was younger. Many of these players were my idols growing up. Now I will be skating alongside them. It is both a weird and an amazing feeling.

Turning my head toward the people surrounding the ice, I notice a television camera crew. They are shooting our warm-ups from ten different angles, interviewing Coach Lewis, and reviewing their notes. I wonder what notes, if any, they have written about me.

Alexi Kornikov skates up behind me and playfully hits me in the back with his stick. "You ready for big time?" he asks.

I nod my head. "I hope so," I tell him.

He drifts backward and smashes the hardest slap shot I have ever seen up close. Amazingly, our goalie, Dave Furion, makes the glove save. He smacks the puck back to Alexi, who passes it over to me. I reach back and take a quick one-timer on goal. My shot is wide right and Furion doesn't even flinch.

Embarrassed by my terrible shot, I race toward the puck near the right boards. With my legs pumping quickly, I show off my speed, which is my greatest strength. I begin to day-dream again, remembering all the hours I spent working on my skating.

The drive home from my middle school tryouts was awful. Mom tried to make me feel better, but every word she uttered did the opposite. "You'll try again next year," she offered. "These things happen, Wayne. Life isn't always fair." Then she paused, adding, "You're bound to grow. And if you don't, that's okay too. You're smart and funny and creative—you can do all kinds of things." It was typical motherly advice. Although I knew it came from her heart, I wished she would just let me be.

As Mom talked, I stared out the window. The conversation became more and more unbearable with every moment. I wanted to tell her that I wasn't giving up on hockey, not by a long shot. Getting cut was a fluke. I didn't get cut because I was a bad player. I was cut because of Darius the Jerk Gray! I couldn't tell her this, though, because I knew that if I did, I would start crying. We rode the rest of the way home in silence.

After we finished a very quiet dinner, I went upstairs to my bedroom. Ricky called me, and I told him all about tryouts, how I was pummeled all over the ice. He told me that I was lucky I got cut, because now I would only have to deal with Darius and his friends at school. We talked for a few more minutes about next year's team and how it would be easier to make, and more fun to be on, with all of the eighth graders off to high school.

For the next hour or so, I tried to block hockey thoughts

from my brain. I ended up doing just the opposite, listening to a Minnesota Elk game on the radio. When Dad knocked on my bedroom door, I quickly flicked it off. I was in bed at this point, flipping my lucky puck into the air, pretending to read my science book. My body ached from the painful collisions I had endured earlier in the day. Still, all I could think about was getting back on the ice.

"Feel like talking about it?" he asked as he slowly opened my door.

"Not really."

Dad sat down on the foot of my bed anyway. He looked up at me and smiled. "Coach Nielson called me. He said you played your heart out." He paused to wait for a response. When there wasn't one, he added, "I'm proud of you."

"I got cut, Dad, did Coach Nielson tell you *that*?"

"He did." Dad paused and then stared deep into my eyes. "Wayne, your Mom and I love you whether or not you play hockey. You know that, right?"

I nodded my head. "Mom already told me all of that stuff." I said. "I've heard it all before. I can be anything I want to be—I know. The problem is that the only thing I want to be is a hockey player." I tossed my lucky puck onto the floor.

Dad reached down and picked it up, staring at it for a few long seconds. "I know what it's like to have a big dream." He took a deep breath, "I guess I just want to tell you that you've got a long road to get there—a hard road. And your dream only dies the day you let it die. If you want today to be that day, that's okay."

"No way," I said. "I'm not quitting."

"Good," Dad smiled, "you're stubborn like your old man. Then don't worry. This is just a bump in the road. If you're really serious about getting there, get ready for a lot more bumps—bigger ones than this. I came real close to my dream, Wayne. I just missed it." Dad smiled again, "I gave it all I had and I'm happy with the way my life turned out. My point is that it's okay if things don't work out the way you plan them. Going for it, though, giving it everything you've got, even when it gets tough like it did today— that's what counts."

I sat up in bed, a few tears rolling down my cheeks. "I love hockey. I love it so much. I just wish I were bigger, like you. If I were—"

Dad reached over and wiped the tears away from my face. "You're not big, though, and crying about not being big isn't gonna make you any bigger." Dad grabbed me by the shoulders as he looked me right in the eyes. "What you've got is this little body, Wayne." He pointed to my chest, "and a big heart. Do the best you can with what you've got."

At this point, I stopped crying. "You're right," I said. I banged my chest with my fist. "This little guy is gonna make it to the NHL."

Dad smiled. "There you go," he said, kissing me on the top of my head before closing my door and saying goodnight.

The next day at four o'clock I showed up at the middle school hockey rink. When I stepped into the locker room and made my way past all the guys who had made the team, my face flushed red. Being there felt strange. Yesterday, we all tried out together, and I got cut. I was sure they were wondering what I was doing there today. I was worried that they would think I was there to beg Coach Nielson for a spot on the team, which wasn't the case.

Taking a deep breath and wiping the sweat off the palms of my hands, I knocked on Coach's office door. He invited me in. During the next few minutes I explained to him that I understood his reasons for cutting me. There were no grudges and no hard feelings. I went on to tell him that despite being cut, I wasn't giving up on my dream. Hockey was too important to me, and I needed to be around the sport. I was coming to him, not to ask for anything, but to offer something: my services as equipment manager.

At first, Coach wasn't sure if he liked the idea. He didn't want me to take on this responsibility only to be frustrated the entire season long. "Are you sure you want to do this?" he asked.

"Absolutely," I said, without hesitation. "Hockey's in my blood. Being around the game can only make me better."

Coach was quiet for a minute or two. "Sit down," he said.

I sat down in the chair on the opposite side of his desk. "I'll do whatever you ask me to, Coach." I looked up at him with eager and hopeful eyes.

"Fine," he said. "But don't ask me for playing time, even during practice. You won't get a jersey, a locker, or even a puck— no special privileges of any kind. You understand me?"

"Yes, Coach."

"You still interested?"

"Yes, no special privileges." I said. "I wouldn't want them. I just want to be around the game. I'll practice on my own time."

"Okay, Miller," he said, "then you're our equipment manager. Be here fifteen minutes before every practice, get the goals set up, water bottles filled, and get the pucks and sticks out. Be fully dressed in skates and pads every day, in case we need a body during practice—which we probably won't."

"Yes, sir," I smiled.

"You want to play in the NHL, right Miller? Well, I'm gonna help you get there. Bring a notebook and a pen to practice—every day. Whatever you notice, I want you to write it down in that notebook. You'll hand it to me at the end of every day. Then we'll talk about it. I promise that this will make you a better player."

"Thank you, Coach. I won't disappoint you. I'll stay out of the way, too." I shook his hand and started for the door. "I'll get that notebook."

"Miller," he shouted, just before I left the room. "Don't quit on me. If you agree to do this, you're agreeing to a full season. If you start up and then quit, don't even bother coming out for the team next year."

"Yes, sir," I said, leaving the room to set everything up for practice.

During the next few months I showed up at every practice about thirty minutes before the guys got there. I suited up, filled all the water bottles, set up the goals, brought out the equipment, and waited for the team to arrive. Occasionally, Coach had me set up cones on the ice for skating drills. Other times, he had me set up only one goal for defensive drills.

Darius and his buddies were relentless in torturing me. From calling me names, to throwing their dirty towels at me, they simply wouldn't leave me alone. I tried my best to ignore them, but sometimes that was impossible. There were more than a few times when Coach had to step in and break up a scuffle between us. I was always thankful when he did.

For the most part, though, the rest of the guys appreciated me being there. I made a bunch of new friends on the team. Coach

Nielson occasionally invited me to participate in practice when one of the guys didn't show up. I savored every chance I got to step on the ice.

Most of the time, however, I wouldn't be on the ice. I would sit on the sidelines with my pen and notebook in hand. At first, I didn't really know what to write, so I jotted down which players hit the hardest slap shots, who skated the fastest, and who was the best at handling the puck. I even ranked every player on the team in these areas. Coach was quick to point out that I was "missing the big picture" and that "all the stats in the world didn't make a great hockey player, and they sure as heck didn't make a great team."

As the season progressed, I started to understand what he meant. I began noticing things about hockey that had escaped me previously. I found that certain guys on our team were more concerned with checking than playing real defense. And when they went for a big check and missed, the entire team broke down defensively. I discovered that most of our passes were more than a foot behind a player who was skating at full speed. When this occurred, fast break opportunities quickly became turnovers. I noted that when our team made at least three solid passes on the offensive end, we almost always got a shot on goal. When we worked together, we were ten times as potent offensively. Finally, I noted that when guys helped each other on defense and didn't get over-aggressive, scoring on us was near impossible. I wrote these things down every day and talked them over with Coach Nielson after practice. Sometimes, I would even bring my notebook home with me and talk about stuff I was seeing with Dad.

I enjoyed taking notes on the game, and I understood why Coach said that my observations would make me a better player.

But don't think for one minute that I didn't want to be on the ice with the team. I couldn't wait until I actually got the chance to put my newfound hockey knowledge to work.

After much begging, Coach gave me a spare key to the rink. Having that key was a responsibility I took very seriously. I was always careful to lock up and turn off all the lights when Mom came to pick me up. When the guys left and Coach went home for the night, I would skate until I could barely move. I skated laps, sprints, and even skated in between and around the orange cones, the way I had seen the team do during practice. Eventually, when I flew around the ice, I was moving so fast that nobody on our team was even close to me at top speed. I found that my small size was an advantage when it came to turning quickly, and changing directions. So I practiced that too. Even though I hadn't made the team, I was skating more than ever before.

Altogether, sixth grade was a great year for me. My feud with Darius was dying down, because the eighth grader was starting to get bored with tormenting me. Ricky and I hung out all the time, and we even made a trip to a Minnesota Elk game, which was awesome. I did really well in school, too, with A's and B's in every subject—even science. And, of course, I improved a lot on the ice. I felt as if I understood the game much better now, and I couldn't wait for my chance to play again.

Little did I know, that with three games left in the season, everything was about to change.

CHAPTER FIVE

BIG BREAK

After finishing warm-ups, all the players line up for the singing of the national anthem. Then we listen as the starting lineups for each team are announced alongside an awesome laser-light show. The special effects at Elk Arena are incredible. I have certainly come a long way from pick-up games.

Finally, we are set to begin the game. Our starting line takes the ice and the crowd begins to pump in the loudest applause of the night. Another NHL season is about to begin. I make my way to the end of the long bench and find a seat. My right arm leans on the edge of the short barrier that separates me from the action of the game. I lean heavily on this barrier, ready to jump over it and go to battle when called upon. My leg shakes up and down—I could not be more excited.

The ref skates out to the middle of the ice, where a few words are being exchanged between the starting centers for each team. I wonder what they are saying to one another as they both prepare for the game's first face-off. As soon as this thought pops into my head, the two men grow intensely quiet, awaiting the puck drop. I lean in closer as they crouch down, ready to flinch the moment the puck hits the ice. The ref skates to within a few feet of the two long-time professionals. He holds the puck high in the air, directly between them—then he drops it.

My mother has always told me that things happen for a reason. I was always sure that mothers said this to their children because they didn't know what else to say when things went wrong. But then something happened that made me start to believe that things really *did* happen for a reason.

A few weeks before the middle school hockey season started—before my cafeteria run-in with Darius Gray, and before I was cut from the team—Mom bumped into Dr. Morris at the supermarket. Dr. Morris has been my doctor since I was a baby. He and Mom got to chatting and he mentioned that a large number of people had recently contracted the flu. This was strange because it was only September, and usually the flu hits Robbinsdale the hardest during winter. Anyway, Mom got worried and made me an appointment for the next day. I remember being annoyed that I had to get a flu shot. As it turned out, that flu shot saved my hockey season.

Apparently, Dr. Morris didn't bump into enough people at the supermarket during the fall, because by the time winter came around, everybody I knew had the flu. Ricky got it so bad that he was in bed for two weeks. Mr. Weathers, my science teacher who always gave me a hard time, got it too. So did Mrs. Smith and Mrs.

Levine, my art teacher and my gym teacher. Even the guy who drove the zambonie, the machine that cleaned the ice at the middle school rink, got sick.

Meanwhile, led by the scoring of Darius Gray, the middle school hockey team was 6-5 heading into the last three games of the season. This meant that they would have to win two of their last three games for a shot at the play-offs. The guys felt as if they had a really good chance. Until, that is, the flu epidemic crippled the team.

The big game against Plymouth Middle School was to be on Tuesday night on our home ice. Coach Nielson scheduled practice at four o'clock on Monday afternoon. As usual, I was there early, setting up. Coach had told me to arrange the cones the way I'd done for skating drills in the past. I remembered what he meant, but I also had a description of the drill he was talking about in my notebook just in case. Before the guys arrived, I had everything ready and was skating through the course myself.

When I looked around the rink just before practice started, I wasn't sure what was happening. The rink was virtually empty. There were supposed to be eighteen players on the team, but with the clock reading just three minutes before four o'clock, only twelve had shown up. This was an all-time low for practice attendance, and Coach Nielson looked worried. He sat in his office talking on the phone. All the while, he chewed on his fingernails nervously.

The team had started to lose some players to the flu last week, and was down to just fifteen guys for last Thursday's game against the Wilson Junior High Soldiers. It appeared as though a few more guys had gone down since then. By 4:15, there were only thirteen players huddled near center ice. Everyone was asking frantic questions to one another: Has anyone heard from Darius? Who else was sick? When were they coming back? How were the guys left standing going to compete against Plymouth?

I was sitting on the sidelines, leaning up in my seat as Coach skated onto the ice to join the guys. With fifteen players, the roster had been very thin against the Soldiers, but with only thirteen, and against the feared team from Plymouth, I wasn't sure how we could compete. If there was ever a time that this team needed me, it was then. My skates were on, my stick was close, and my heart was racing.

"Okay, fellas, gather round and be quiet," Coach tried to speak over the panicked voices of a worried group of hockey players. "Just calm down!" He yelled. The guys stopped talking and formed a tight circle around Coach. "How's everybody feeling?" Coach looked around at each player, one at a time. "Anybody have a scratchy throat, feeling hot, anything like that?"

The guys shook their heads, one by one. "Good, then we've got thirteen healthy guys for tomorrow's game." Coach said. "As I'm sure you all know, everybody in this town seems to have gotten the flu. Darius's got it, Craig's got it, and I just spoke to Brock's Mom—he's got it too. Mike, Jesse and Nick are getting better, but they'll be out for tomorrow's game, and maybe Thursday's." Coach cleared his throat. "Right now, we need to be a team more than ever." He turned around and faced me. Then he took a loud, deep breath. "Wayne, drop your notebook, and get over here."

He didn't have to ask me twice. Before he finished his sentence, I was skating toward the team at full speed. I assumed that they needed me to run through some of the drills with them. Having an extra body out there would be a big help.

What I found out, though, was that Coach wasn't simply looking for a body. Suddenly, and very matter-of-factly, he said, "Wayne's on the team for the rest of the year. You've all played with him. He hustles, he's quick, he's got heart, and he got a flu shot. Welcome aboard, Miller—we're glad to have you." I smiled. I'd gotten my big break. Now I just had to take advantage of it.

The reaction I got from the guys was mixed. I heard a few guys clap but I also heard a few sigh. I even heard a "not Miller" comment.

"Okay, guys, line up for some skating. Wayne, come over here," Coach Nielson blew his whistle. I skated over to him, and the rest of the team formed a line behind the cones. He grabbed me by the jersey I wore and spoke in a loud voice, "You earned this. Don't let anybody tell you different."

"Yes, sir," I said.

"Now get in line!"

I skated over to the rest of the team. Coach drifted toward the opposite end of the cones course, which extended about three quarters of the way down the ice. The cones were set up about ten feet apart from one another, which meant there was no chance of reaching full speed. This drill was all about agility and quickness. At the end of the course, Coach had dropped a puck, which was about fifteen feet from the goal. When a player reached the puck, he was supposed to shoot it in. Coach held a stopwatch in his hand and was timing us. There were a few rules: If you knocked over a cone, five seconds were added to your time; if you missed the shot, ten seconds were added.

One at a time, guys skated through the course, reached the puck, and took a shot on goal. Some made it, some missed, a few knocked over a cone or two, others took it slow and steady. I was last in line. I waited patiently for my turn as each player finished the course. With only two guys standing in front of me, I started to get antsy. I couldn't help but imagine myself ripping through the course and setting the day's record. Other brash thoughts ran through my brain: *When the guys see my speed, they're going to be so impressed that they'll have no choice but to accept me as a teammate.*

For now, I had to deal with some doubters. "Way to sneak your way onto the team. You'll screw this up for sure." Javier Cervantes spoke into my ear, just before taking off on his run through the course. Javier was the last of Darius's friends not to contract the flu and was one of a handful of guys who looked annoyed by my presence on the team.

Before I could think too much about it, Javier finished his run. "Miller, you're up," Coach shouted, blowing his whistle and clicking on his stopwatch.

I took off immediately, tearing through the course at a record pace. My skates felt as if they were a part of my feet. The ice was fast and I was cutting corners with the precision of a surgeon. My legs barely brushed the cones as I passed them. I was as light as a feather, and as smooth as the ice I glided on. With five cones behind me, I was staring down a perfect run. At this point, I was confident that I would achieve the best time of the day.

With just two cones left, I began to focus on the puck. To be as fast as possible, I planned on shooting while skating, and never slowing down. I'd done this before, and although it wasn't easy, I was sure I could do it again. In a few seconds, the shocked expressions on the faces of my teammates would tell the story. The equipment manager was about to have the best run of the day!

I pumped my legs and sped toward the final cone, changing directions quickly in order to angle myself for a shot on goal. I was moving so fast that when I dug the edge of my skate into the ice to stop my momentum, a spray of snow flew into the air. Never slowing down, I turned to face the goal. When I'd just about reached the puck, I began my backswing.

Lifting my stick into the air behind my head made me lose my balance ever so slightly. Instead of regaining my balance and setting up for the shot, I tried to take the shot while falling. Of course, this was a bad idea. When I swung at the puck, I never touched it. My stick hit the ice, followed by my body. I could hear my teammates snickering behind me as I bit down on my tongue.

"You're out of control, Miller." Coach was quick to point out. I hung my head, knowing that I had wasted a golden opportunity to make a good impression.

While the guys were in the shower after practice, I cleaned up the cones and put away the goals. Coach came out of his office and told me that I could hit the showers—that he would take care of the equipment now that I was on the team. Continuing to grab the cones, I insisted that I finish what I had started. After all, I made a commitment to him for the season, and I planned on honoring it. Besides, I wasn't exactly looking forward to facing my teammates.

The next morning before school, I packed my uniform into my backpack and tried to put my big spill behind me. That night, we would be playing a big game against Plymouth—my first as a member of the team. With only fourteen of us on the roster, I knew that I was going to see plenty of ice time. This thought excited me. Unfortunately, I was sure that my teammates had little confidence in my abilities—especially after yesterday's practice. I had a lot to prove against Plymouth and I knew it.

The game started with me on the bench. Even though I was nervous, being a part of the team was an amazing feeling. Our first line was giving Plymouth all they could handle early on. Although I had attended every game this season, I found myself cheering louder than ever now that I was in uniform.

About six minutes into the first period, the puck was slapped down the boards into our opponent's territory and we quickly changed lines. Coach put me in at right wing. The moment I skated onto the ice, I realized that the game was a little different than I had remembered it from elementary school. Or maybe it was me that was different. Either way, it seemed like the players were moving around quicker and the puck was harder to keep track of. I skated around like crazy during the next few minutes, but never got my stick on it.

I did land a pretty solid check on a Plymouth forward who was coming into our zone on the break. For a little guy, my check packed a mean punch. Their forward lost his balance and fell to the ground, losing the puck in the process. Overall, it was a great start to my season, albeit a late start.

Coach slapped my helmet as I made my way back onto the bench a couple of minutes later, "way to play tough defense, Miller." His comment was music to my ears.

I sat down on the bench and awaited my next opportunity to play. I didn't have to wait long. A few minutes later, I was back out there. This time, my aim was to really impress Coach Nielson and my teammates. I skated into position on the right side of the ice. The same forward who I had checked during my last bit of playing time was skating right at me with the puck. There was no way I could check him from the angle I was at, so I went for a stick poke, but missed by a long shot. He made a nice move, switching hands and faking me out of my skates.

Oh, no, I thought. *I just gave them a fast break!* As I tried to recover, they made a few quick passes that led to a short slap shot, which just snuck past the glove of our goalie, Jack Nix. That quickly, my mistake cost us a goal. It was 1-0 Plymouth.

When I got to the bench, I heard a couple of guys talking about my miscue. Coach Nielson saw that I was upset at the end of the bench, and made his way over to me. "Wayne, if you lose your confidence you can't help this team. Make up for it on your next shift. Remember what we talked about—don't get overaggressive, let the game come to you." This advice was exactly what I needed to hear. I picked my head up and realized that I was simply trying too hard. I knew this game. Forcing things never made for good hockey.

When I came back in at the end of the second period, I was a completely different player. I was no longer searching for the puck, trying to make a play. Instead, I was focused on my part of the ice, my territory. I drifted backwards when my opponent's pushed up. My conservative, fundamentally sound defense, forced Plymouth to make more passes to cross into our zone.

With four minutes left in the period, I got my first big opportunity. Staying back on defense to contain, I waited for their right wing to enter my zone. On the previous two plays, he had waited until he reached the blue line to pass back across the ice to his center. As he skated toward the blue line again, I got ready to pounce. Sure enough, he made it to the blue line and decided to pass back to the middle. Anticipating his pass, I took off.

I was able to cut off the puck and make a break for the goal. Once I had controlled it, I made a nice crossover move on their center, leaving him in the dust. Because their defensemen had been pushing up with their forwards, they had no chance of recovering. They were drifting backwards when I was reaching full speed at their blue line. I sped past them easily. I had never skated like that before. I was like a flash of lightning.

Before I knew it, I was fifteen feet from the goal, with nobody between myself and the goalie. As the goalie flinched to his left on my fake, I moved the puck to my backhand, and poked one in from about five feet away. Goal! Tie score!

Scoring that goal was the greatest feeling I had ever felt on the ice. It's not that I'd never scored a goal before. I had been a top scorer for my team the year before, but I had never worked so hard or waited so patiently for an opportunity. It had taken me two months to get here, and as I scored, I realized that it was worth it.

My teammates circled me in celebration. Even Javier Cervantes gave me a chest bump. For the first time, I was no longer the equipment manager—I was a part of the team.

With my confidence soaring, I scored again three plays later. And near the end of the third period, I hit a slap shot that ricocheted off the goalie's glove and went in. It was my third goal of the game, and the first hat-trick of my life. I was the star of the game as we beat Plymouth 3 to 1, staying alive in the play-off hunt.

CHAPTER SIX

TEAMMATES

When I woke up this morning I felt confident that I was completely prepared for the speed and power of an NHL game. After all, I've watched hundreds of games on television, and I've sat in the stands at a handful of Elk games as well. But sitting here on the bench, just a few feet away from the action, I'm seeing things differently. These guys are faster than anything I imagined. Plus, they all seem to be built like trucks. I'm starting to wonder if my speed, which has been an asset for me since the first time I put on skates, will even be a factor against these guys. This thought scares me for a second, and I wonder: if I'm not the fastest guy out there, but I'm still the smallest, then where's my edge?

Just as this thought passes through my head, Coach Lewis screams over to me. "Miller, get in there!"

The puck is smacked along the boards toward the far end of the ice, and I jump out of my seat with my heart beating through my chest. A second later, I am playing in an NHL game. Strangely, the moment my skates touch the ice, everything feels okay. I realize that, yes, I do belong here. The only feeling I can compare it to is the feeling of coming home—I am at home on the ice.

I keep my eye on the puck as I drift back on defense. The small black disc is being passed around the Firestorm's zone quickly and efficiently. The whooshing sound it makes as it hovers over the ice is unmistakable. Each whoosh is followed by a smack, as the puck makes contact with the center of a wooden stick. It's the sound of a perfect pass, and it's music to my ears. Dad used to tell me that only true hockey players were able to appreciate the subtle noises of the game. These noises have never been clearer to me than they are right now—with the game being played at such a high level.

I don't dare push up into the Firestorm's zone, as I am waiting for the rest of my line to get into position. One overaggressive move on this stage, and a rookie like me can be made to look very bad in a hurry. Finally, our line is set, so I skate forward on the attack, pressuring the defense a bit. Unlike high school or college hockey, these defensemen are virtually unaffected by my pressure. Still, I skate quickly toward them.

I no longer look like a burst of lightning on the ice—it's not that I have slowed down: the men I am playing with are simply much quicker than the competition in high school and college. I imagine that I still look pretty fast to them, but I am sure that my speed is not what they notice right now. More likely, they notice that I am young, overmatched, overwhelmed—and tiny.

The puck moves around behind the Firestorm's goal. Our right wing, George McClain, goes after it with a sudden burst. He lays a nice check on a Firestorm defender, who quickly smacks the puck around the boards and into our zone. I drift back again, until I am standing alone on the right side of center ice. For the moment, I appear to be open. Before I even realize this, a sharp pass comes toward me. I await it, looking up the ice, ready to make a run. The instant the puck makes contact with my stick, a blur of red and black smashes into me. He leads with his shoulder and blasts me back into the boards. I slump to my knees, and can hear the fans oohing and aahing behind me. Not only do I lose the puck, but my stick as well.

Luckily, our defense grabs the loose puck, smacking it back down the boards. With my entire body in shock from the hardest hit I have ever taken, I grab my stick off the ice and clumsily skate back to the bench for another line change.

Everything changed for me after my performance against Plymouth. When I stepped into that locker room after the game, I really felt like I was a part of the team. More important, the guys treated me different. Scoring three goals in a hockey game had earned me their respect.

In a weird twist, I found myself spending a lot of time hanging out with Javier. Even though we had been at odds with each other early on in the year, I found that the eighth grader was a really good guy. Sure, he hung out with Darius and sometimes acted like a bully, but he was quick with an apology and I was just as quick to forgive him. He confessed that he had actually felt bad for me when Darius was pouring food on my head in the cafeteria. Although he had wanted to step in and say something at the time, he explained that even though he was bigger and stronger than Darius, standing up to the bully was a hard thing to do. I understood exactly what he was saying.

Being friends with the biggest guy on the team, not to mention the biggest guy in our entire middle school, was pretty cool. But there was something happening out on the ice that was even cooler: I was making dramatic improvements. It seemed like every day I was taking another big step. During practice, I was emerging as a quiet leader, giving an all-out effort on every play and pushing my teammates to do the same.

By the following week, our depleted roster started to fill in again as a few more guys came back from their battles with the flu. Darius was still sick, though. Strangely, the seventeen of us who remained started to gel in a way we hadn't with Darius on the ice. There was no more fear of looking stupid, and no more worrying about Darius getting angry when he didn't touch the puck. In light of his absence, we began to play as a team, no longer relying on the talented eighth grader to carry us on his back. The results were amazing. Not only did we win the next two games after beating Plymouth, but we outscored our opponents 11 to 2! In doing so, we qualified for the playoffs with a record of 9-5 on the season.

During the two weeks of practice since I'd joined the team, I really worked hard. Reading through my notebook every night, I recalled several conversations I'd had with Coach Nielson. I made sure that when I stepped onto the ice, I was doing all the little things he told me would make me a great hockey player. As a result, my passing was sharp, and I was consistently skating with my head up, finding teammates when they had opportunities. I discovered that I had a natural talent for passing, and that while I could make a shot, I was much more dangerous when I was passing.

At the same time, though, I had been focusing on the development of my backhanded shot. This improved shot allowed me to score more consistently when I was around the goal with the puck. Dad had always told me that to be a great passer, the defense must respect your ability to score. Otherwise they will look for the pass every time, and have an easy time cutting it off. If they have to prevent you from scoring as well, then you have them on their heels.

Darius Gray joined us during our last practice before the big game. Just as quickly as we'd come together, we fell apart. First of all, he was not happy to see that I was on the roster. I still get chills when I remember the look he gave me the first day he saw me suited up on the ice. Because of his animosity toward me, my game fell to pieces. I was definitely part of the reason the team struggled when Darius returned. I was totally intimidated by Darius's presence, and once again, was trying too hard to make plays. I became overly aggressive, leaving my territory defensively and taking wild shots. I knew that if I made mistakes like these during tomorrow's game, I would cost us dearly.

Of course, Darius was right there to point out my short-comings on the ice, along with the shortcomings of our teammates. He was so vocal in his criticism that many players turned into statues on the ice. Not wanting to be called out by Darius, guys who were making plays just a few days earlier seemed to completely disappear. The moment they touched the puck, they would be searching for Darius. Once they found him, they would force a pass in to him, regardless of the situation.

Javier was one of these guys. When Darius was in bed sick, Javier played the role of enforcer, making sure that nobody from the opposing team reached the middle of our zone without getting clocked. He was absolutely awesome during our last three games. Watching him in practice, though, you would think he was only there to make sure that nobody on the opposing team got near Darius. He looked slow, sluggish, and completely out of sync. With Darius back, we were a team in complete disarray.

That night after practice, I met Ricky down at the arcade in the Brookville Mall. I talked to him about the way the team was playing now that Darius was back. I told him that I was really worried about our upcoming game. He said that there was probably nothing I could do, and that I should just wait until next year when Darius was off to high school. I laughed, telling him that we were going to change his nickname from Quick Rick to Scared Stiff Rick. He laughed, too, but punched me in the arm pretty hard anyway.

We ate some ice cream and played video games for the next hour—Ricky even set the record on the mini basketball pop-a-shot machine. He was unbelievable at that game. It seemed like he never missed. I told him that he should go out for the basketball team next year, and he was seriously thinking about it. Not only could he shoot the lights out, but while I seemed to remain the same height year after year, Ricky was growing like a weed.

We were in the middle of our fifth game in a row when I saw Javier coming over to us. He was with a few girls that I recognized from school. When Ricky saw them, his grip tightened on the basketball he was holding, and he tried to stand behind me. It probably looked pretty funny—Ricky hiding behind me, and me only as tall as his shoulders.

Before Ricky could bolt, Javier called out. "What's happening, Wayne?" He slapped my hand and I introduced Javier to Ricky, who looked completely shocked when the eighth grader gave him a head nod in recognition. The girls Javier walked in with were also eighth graders—two beauties who were *way* out of our league. Just as Javier was about to introduce us, I noticed Darius walking toward us. I knew right away that this was going to be trouble.

Darius came toward me like he was about to check me into the boards, only there weren't any boards—just a giant pop-a-shot machine, two eighth-grade girls, Scared Stiff Ricky, and Javier. "Look who it is, our team mascot and his nerdy friend." Darius laughed loudly at his joke. "Honestly, you guys are the stupidest looking pair I've ever seen." He walked up to Ricky and laughed in his face. "This guy's as tall as house and as skinny as a stick," then he came up to me, "and I can barely even see this little geek. You look like an elf, Miller."

Ricky whispered to me right away, "Let's go, Wayne. I don't feel like getting—"

"Hey, Darius," I said, playing off his comment and ignoring Ricky's plea for us to leave. "Always good to see you, buddy— have a nice night." After I made my sarcastic comment, I turned around and pretended Darius wasn't there.

"I'm not your buddy," he muttered under his breath.

I barely heard him, as I had already turned my back and started talking to Javier again. "Check this out, Javier," I said, pulling a small bag from my pocket. "I got new laces for my skates— blue and white."

"Team colors. Cool." Javier said. "You know what I thought

would be cool? If we all cut our hair like—"

Darius cut Javier off, putting his hand on the big defensemen's shoulder and pulling him away from me. "We? Why are you saying "we" to this loser, Javier? He's not one of us, he's the equipment manager. If we didn't all get sick he'd still be filling our water bottles and picking up our towels. Think about it." Darius walked right up to me and got in my face. "Don't think I'm going to treat you any different just because you weaseled your way onto the team, Miller." He accentuated his sentence by spitting angrily on the ground, barely missing my shoe.

His comment hurt my feelings at first, but then I realized something: "Maybe you haven't heard, Darius, but since you got sick, we've won three games in a row. Think about that." After I said these menacing words I turned my back on Darius again. Then I stuck another quarter into the pop-a-shot machine.

When I wasn't looking, Darius came running at me. I didn't see him coming until the last second. Instinctively, I lowered my shoulder and bent my knees, as if I were about to absorb a check on the ice. I waited for impact, closing my eyes and hoping that no bones would break as I smashed into the pop-a-shot machine, which stood right behind me. But just before Darius reached me, Javier stepped in front of him, stopping him in his tracks and knocking him to the ground.

"What the heck are you doing, Javier?" Darius screamed, brushing himself off and trying to get past the monster frame of his former tag team partner. There was no way to move Javier, and Darius knew it. Instead of fighting his friend, he screamed at him. "Forget you—you traitor! If you want to hang out with this little weasel then you go ahead. I'm out of here!" Darius said, as he stormed out of the arcade.

I let out a deep and long sigh of relief as I slapped Javier on the back appreciatively. If not for him blocking Darius, I would have been leveled. Although my first instinct was relief, it was short-lived. My emotions changed faster than an NHL slap-shot. I quickly began to worry about our big game the next day. Like it or not, Darius was the best player on our team, and represented our best chance of winning. I was only a sixth-grader, one of two twelve-year-olds on the team. I would give it my best shot, but we were going to need everyone to play their best if we wanted to win the section.

The following afternoon was the first playoff game. We were facing Sandburg Middle School, the team that won our section last year. The players from Golden Valley had finished the regular season with the same record as we did—nine wins and five losses. They were definitely an intimidating group, because many of them were on last year's championship team. We hadn't even made the playoffs last year, so this was our first experience in a "do-or-die" game.

I started that game on the bench, and Darius took back his position on the first line. Right from the start of that game, we weren't playing as a unit. Everyone was standing around and watching Darius. He was definitely an incredible player—probably the best on the ice. But he hogged the puck and consistently took on two or three defenders instead of passing. We played one on five out there, and even with the best player, we were totally outmatched.

Within a few minutes, Sandburg scored their first goal of the game. I was on the second line and entered the game just after that. While I skated after loose pucks and hustled back to play defense, Darius sat on the bench and pouted. The line I played with gave Sandburg all they could handle for the next ten minutes, and the score remained 1-0. As the first period reached the halfway mark, my line was replaced by our third line. I skated to the bench and sat down a few seats away from Darius, who no longer spoke to me, or to Javier, after the incident at the arcade.

The first period came to an end, and Coach put Darius's line in to start the second. Once again, our offense was stagnant when our star player was on the ice. He managed to get one decent shot on goal, but his defense was just terrible. He hung around in the opponent's zone the entire time. Predictably, Sandburg struck again and took a 2-0 lead.

Coach immediately called a timeout and huddled us all together. "Let's start playing like a team out there. Make the extra pass, help each other on defense. Come on, guys!" He looked over at Darius when he said, "One guy can't win this—we have to play together." Coach scratched his head, before saying, "Wayne, get in at left wing, Darius you stay in with the second line." He looked at both of us, making it obvious that he could feel the tension between us. "Help each other—you're teammates. You guys can be a dynamic duo if you stop being cry babies and get used to each other. You don't have to be best friends, but be teammates!"

I looked over at Darius, who rolled his eyes at me. Then he bumped into me as we skated onto the ice. "Stay out of my way."

So much for being teammates, I thought.

Right from the face-off, it appeared that Coach Nielson's experiment was going to be a disaster. Darius continued to hog the puck, making sure to never even look in my direction. It seemed like nothing could bring us together.

While Darius was skating near center ice, I trailed him, hoping he would drop the puck back to me for a clear shot on goal. So far, I had no such luck. As I skated about fifteen feet behind him, I noticed a defensive player charging him from the right boards. I could tell that Darius didn't see him coming. When I saw the guy break, I started to skate as fast as I could to stop him. I knew that if Darius were blindsided, he would lose the puck, and Sandburg would have a fast break. Although part of me wanted to see him get leveled, I knew that Darius going down wouldn't be good for our team.

Just before the defensive player reached Darius the Jerk I lunged toward him, giving up my body for my teammate. My small-ish frame collided with the defensive player's body and we both tumbled to the ground. Darius turned around just in time to see the collision take place. He took advantage of the open right side of the ice. He skated to his right, past a slower defender, and fired in a slap shot that tickled the back of the net.

I was still lying on the ice, having a tough time getting to my feet because the wind had been knocked out of me. But I saw the goal go in and I raised my fist high into the air. Turning to face me, Darius skated back from the goal. When he was just above me, he reached out his hand and helped me to my feet. "Thanks, Wayne."

"We're teammates, Darius. You don't have to thank me."

"Thanks anyway." Darius shook my hand. "Let's win this!" he said. That was as close as anyone would ever get to an apology from Darius.

I smiled, knowing that his days of pushing me around were likely over.

The rest of the game was an absolute blur of excitement.

Trailing Sandburg by a goal, Darius and I went on the offensive every time we were on the ice together. Coach was right, we *were* a dynamic duo. My speed, coupled with his power and big shot, were a deadly combination. By the end of that game I had scored a goal and had three assists. As a team, we scored five more times and went on to win by a final of 6-3.

The next game was the finals, and we played a team that was ranked in the state that year. They were great at every position. Not surprisingly, we lost. But we played well, taking the game into overtime, before falling 1-0. That game marked the last time I would ever have to play with Darius. He went on to high school the following year, and his family moved to California the year after that. By the time I started high school, Darius Gray was a distant memory.

CHAPTER SEVEN

TIME FLIES

I am back on the bench as the final seconds of the first period tick away. After absorbing that hit a few minutes earlier, I am struggling to get rid of the cobwebs in my head. Everything is spinning—I feel like a piece of clothing that has just gone through the washing machine.

When the first period ends, Alexi Kornikov sits beside me on the bench. "You took big hit, huh?"

"I'm all right," I say, rolling my neck so that it cracks. "I never saw that guy coming."

"Sometimes big hit wake you up!" he says, shaking my shoulder forcefully.

I smile at him as he jumps over the boards with the rest of the first line. We are about to begin the second period. "I'm up now!" I call out, as he moves into position at left wing.

The second period is a defensive struggle, just as the first was. Neither team is getting any clean shots. Both offenses continue to play conservatively. In most NHL games, this style of play eventually begins to change as the game progresses. At some point, talented offensive players become restless and attack their opponents despite the risk of a counterattack.

With twelve minutes left in the second, we are called for a penalty. It's hooking on John Simpson, and he yells at the ref as if he's innocent. Simpson never goes down without a fight—even when it comes to the refs. He makes his way over to the penalty box, and Coach quickly calls over his penalty-killing line from the bench. Before he sends them in, though, he pulls out Nick Brolefski.

Then he looks over at me and yells, "Miller, get in at right wing. Show us some speed, kid." Before he can even finish his sentence, I am out on the ice. To be honest, I am completely shocked that I have been called into the game with this line.

For two minutes, Chicago will have five players on the ice, and we will only have four. This is a tremendous opportunity for our opponents. It is also a huge responsibility for me during my first professional game—I take the responsibility as a compliment from Coach Lewis. He obviously thinks that my speed is important, and will be useful, with one man down. Many coaches like to have their biggest guys on the ice to kill penalties. Apparently, Coach Lewis sees things differently. His penalty-killing line is made up of three giants, plus me—the small speedy guy. My job is to be everywhere all at once.

When I get out on the ice, I am pumped. Five Firestorm players come at us right away on the attack. They spread out in our zone, knowing that their one-man advantage will al-

ways leave someone uncovered. I do my best to identify open lanes and cut them off. The first pass is made deep into the corner. I am focused on the puck, unwilling to take my eyes off of it—even for a second. Our right defenseman, Craig Smith, makes a big check on a Firestorm forward, gains possession of the puck, and then hammers it along the boards. That play will buy us about fifteen seconds. Then they'll be back on the attack. I reposition myself near center ice along the right boards.

Before I can even catch my breath, they're coming at us again. Their center makes a quick pass over to the wing and I stand tall (well, as tall as I can) to face him. He fakes a pass back to center, but I don't flinch. I hold my ground. Then he fires a pass back to a defenseman who trails him. Instead of waiting around, I attack. The defenseman sees me coming and tries to pass it back to the right wing for a four-on-three break. But I intercept his pass and begin skating toward the goal with the puck. The crowd gets loud as they are about to witness a one-on-one showdown with the goalie.

The rest of middle school passed in the blink of an eye. I played on the hockey team as a seventh grader, and once again we qualified for the playoffs. That season was a lot of fun for me, especially because this time I was on the team from the beginning. Although we lost in the second round of the playoffs, it was a successful season. That year turned out to be even more fun because Ricky was on the team. He was solid on skates and his slap shot was awesome. When he swung his long arms back and then forward, the puck shot off his stick like a cannon. It was really fun having my best friend on the team.

The other amazing thing that happened during my seventh grade year was that I grew a few inches. When I put my back against the wall in my bedroom on the first day of school, I was shocked! The pencil mark I made on the wall was a full three inches above last year's mark. That was the most I had ever grown in one year.

By the time eighth grade came around, I had grown another few inches. At thirteen years old, I stood four feet nine. I was certainly no giant, but at least I wasn't the shortest kid in school. It helped that as an eighth grader, many kids were a year or two younger than me. But still, I wasn't the shortest, and it felt great.

Ricky quit the hockey team, though, so that kind of stunk. He had turned into a real star on the basketball court at this point, so he focused on that sport instead. My best friend now stood over six feet tall, towering over me by more than a foot. I joked around with him sometimes about being so tall. I usually referred to him as Godzilla, and would remove the padding from his shoes when I was at his house and he wasn't looking. This way, I explained to him, I wouldn't have to look like I was his kid brother.

As an experienced eighth grader, I was elected captain of the hockey team. I had a great season, earning the MVP award when our season ended. I was an assist-machine that year, averaging close to two per game. Although I scored eight goals that season, too, I was much more proud of my twenty-six assists. I led the entire league! The guy who finished second only had twelve.

I had really found my comfort zone on the ice, and I owed a lot of that to Coach Nielson. As I entered high school, where the competition really stiffened, the hardest thing for me to do was leave my coach. Luckily, under his tutelage, I was well aware of my strengths—and my weaknesses too. Coach had always told us that knowing the kind of hockey players we were was the most important way for us to be successful. He explained that great teams didn't have twenty guys with great slap shots, or twenty guys who could really check—great teams had guys who all contributed in different ways.

When I finished middle school, I knew exactly what I did well: I was a speedy skater, a deadly passer, and a great defensive player. I planned on taking these skills with me to high school and building on them.

I made the junior varsity team as a freshman, which was a pretty big deal because only one other freshman made it. Coach Nielson put in a good word for me with Coach Peters, the JV coach, so I made the team despite a mediocre tryout. Being a freshman was tough. During eighth grade, I felt like the king of the middle school. I had tons of friends, was captain of the hockey team, and was older than most of the kids at school. When I got to high school, though, all of that changed. Some of the guys on my team had beards and moustaches, they drove their cars to practice, and most of them had girlfriends. I couldn't grow facial hair, I was two years away from getting my license, and I'd only been on one date.

I managed to survive freshman year without too many problems. I knew some of the upperclassmen from playing with them on the middle school hockey team, like Javier. He was a junior and bigger than ever. Having him on my side definitely made my transition a little easier. Still, hanging out with the guys on the JV team was pretty much all I did socially. That, and spending time with Ricky and a few guys he'd met on the basketball team. Academically, I was doing just fine. In fact, my first semester of high school also marked the first time that I earned a 4.0. Mom and Dad were so excited that they bought me a brand new pair of skates—the only present I ever asked for.

When sophomore year began, things got easier for me. I grew another inch and easily made the varsity team after playing amazing hockey during tryouts. We had a decent team that year, but I still managed to make my way onto the first line. Being on the starting line was something I was really proud of. At fifteen, I stood at five foot three. Once again, I was the smallest guy on the team. At that point, though, I was used to it. If I ever felt bad about being so short, I thought back to what my father had told me after I'd gotten cut from my middle school team: "What you've got is this little body, Wayne. And a big heart. Do the best you can with what you've got." From that day on, I had.

We reached the sectional finals that year but were destroyed by Roosevelt 6-0. I played terribly during that final contest, which made me twice as motivated to work on my game that summer.

I spent every free moment I had during July and August working on getting into top physical shape. For a hockey player trying to get a college scholarship, it is all about your junior and senior years. I knew this coming season was my first big chance to show the college scouts that I could play. Unfortunately, I had one big strike against me—my size. Nobody wanted to give a scholarship to a guy as small as me. If I had any chance of getting a free ride to college, I would need to take my game to the next level.

Instead of joining a gym, like several of my teammates had—I worked out the old-fashioned way. I ran ten miles every morning when I woke up. Then, at night, I went down to Mickey's Ice Arena and scrimmaged with the older men. They would play in shifts, but I asked that I never be taken off the ice. This was my way of pushing myself to the limit. What the old guys lacked in speed, they made up for with hockey knowledge. I even got the chance to play alongside my forty-nine-year-old father that summer. Although he was a step slower, he still showed some flashes of greatness. I learned a lot from playing with him.

The physically demanding schedule I put myself through got me in the best shape of my life. Most of the guys I knew who were gearing up for their runs at a scholarship, spent their summer drinking protein shakes and lifting weights. My strategy was entirely different. Going with what Coach Nielson had taught me, I played to my strengths. I was never going to be big, no matter how many shakes I drank or weights I lifted. So I focused my energy on making myself faster. My goal—and I know this sounds crazy—was to be the fastest hockey player in the world. I knew that if I was the fastest guy they'd ever seen, coaches and scouts would be forced to ignore my size—because ignoring my speed would be impossible.

When hockey season started during my junior year, our team was stacked. *The Post*, our town's local paper, picked us to win the section. That was something our high school hadn't been able to accomplish in a long time. There was an article in the paper a week before the season started under the headline "Riding Little Wayne." It was all about how I was going to make or break the season with my playmaking ability. It definitely put some pressure on me, but I was proud of it. I cut it out and hung it on my wall. I was happy that I was recognized as the key to success on a team filled with talented players—even if they wanted to call me Little Wayne, a nickname I had never been able to completely come to terms with.

Early on, the paper's prediction turned out to be right on target. We won our first five games of the season and I was playing better than ever. My workout regimen during the summer made me much faster, and allowed me to keep skating while other players tired and weakened. My size became less of a factor with my increased speed because I was pretty hard to hit. Players trying to check me often whiffed as I skated past them. I even heard one coach telling his guys *not* to check me. He was afraid they would miss and give us a fast break.

By mid-December my mailbox was filled with recruiting letters from colleges. Coaches from major hockey programs around the country were writing and asking me to come visit their schools. Although it was too early to receive any phone calls from them, let alone formal offers, I was starting to get excited about the possibilities. If I continued to improve, I was going to be playing Division I hockey.

Of course, the only school I really wanted to attend was Minnesota College. The Silver Snakes had one of the most respected hockey programs in the country. Growing up, I had always been a big fan. Naturally, there were other schools that I would have liked to play for as well. But growing up in Minnesota, the Snakes represented the pinnacle of collegiate hockey to me.

In the middle of that season, I got an exciting letter from Minnesota College's assistant coach, Pete Mitchum. The letter said that Minnesota College had taken notice of me. It went on to say that they would be monitoring my progress during this summer and into next hockey season. I couldn't have been more excited. The Silver Snakes were interested in me!

After that letter arrived, I became a little obsessed with searching for scouts. When I skated onto the ice before every game I checked the stands for them. My father would constantly remind me to stay focused on the game and ignore the people in the stands. Besides, he would tell me, even if I saw a scout, that didn't necessarily mean he was scouting me. Still, it was impossible not to look.

The rest of that season went really well. We finished with a record of 12 and 2, which matched the best record our high school ever had. The last time we had even managed to win 10 games was the year we had two All-Americans, both of whom are now NHL players. After cruising through the first two rounds of the playoffs, we barely lost the section to Wayzata High School in a 2 to 1 game that was one of the more exciting I've ever played in. I scored our lone goal, but it wasn't enough. Losing was disappointing, but with most of the guys on our squad returning next year for their senior seasons, I was sure we would have a chance to win the entire thing.

The first game of our senior season was against our rivals, Copper River High School. They notoriously played a rough game, relying on the size of their players, rather then their speed. Although they rarely contended for the section, playing them was always a tough game.

I got off to a great start by scoring a quick goal just two minutes into the game. Skating down the right side, I was able to avoid a large defender and stick the puck between the legs of their goalie on a backhanded effort. That gave us a 1 to 0 lead against a team that had a hard time scoring. We took off from there, scoring another goal in the second period, and a third goal to start the third.

With seven minutes remaining in the game, I skated onto

the ice for a line change. I had no idea that my entire life was about to change.

Getting into position on the right side of the ice, I waited for their offense to push up. They did, and the pressure put on by our left wing, caused an errant pass. Right when I saw that the puck was loose, I darted across the middle of the ice. With my legs pumping and my skates pushing against the ice, I took off. I chased down that loose puck the same way I had been chasing down loose pucks my whole life—with everything I had.

The puck was near the boards, so I stopped sharply once I reached it, shooting snow high into the air. My back was to their goal and I stared down at the black disc, trying to kick it with my skate. I couldn't smack it with my stick because I was being hooked by a defender and our stick's had tangled. He had arrived on the scene a moment earlier. He was close enough to me for his grunting to be loud in ears. I fought him off with everything I had, even though he was much stronger than me. Finally, I was able to get a blade on the puck, kicking it into the middle of the ice like a soccer player.

Just as I was following through with my kick, though, I saw a second defenseman coming right at me. He was about to reach me, but tripped and fell. As he came crashing toward me, there was nothing I could do but wait for impact.

My left leg, which was in the air at this point, was the only thing that broke his fall. His body landed awkwardly, with my leg absorbing the full weight of his 200-pound frame. I fell to the ground with him on top of me and my leg bent back in a strange way. Right away, I screamed. "My leg! My leg!" A sharp pain like nothing I had ever felt before shot through my body like a bolt of lightning.

Seeing me flipping around on the ice in pain, coach raced out to me. He helped to carry me to the sidelines. The pain in my left leg was unbearable. Soon after that, I was placed in an ambulance and rushed to North Memorial Medical Center.

When I arrived at the emergency room, it took them just ten minutes to tell me that my leg had been badly broken. It took me thirty minutes to stop crying when I realized that my season was over and that my leg might never be the same again.

Mom and Dad had both been at the game, but they had to drive to the hospital separate from the ambulance. They arrived a few minutes after the doctor began casting my leg. Mom didn't speak when she came over. Instead she squeezed my hand and looked into my eyes with a pained expression that belongs only to mothers worried about their children's health. Her soft kiss on my head did nothing to ease my pain, or hers.

With tears welled up in his eyes, Dad stared over at my leg. He paced around the room in large circles and asked every doctor within ten feet a thousand different questions. But he didn't dare look at my eyes. Somehow, I knew that he just couldn't bear to. This wound was eerily similar to the one he had suffered through. The pain I was feeling was a pain he knew all too well—and I don't mean the pain in my leg. The last time he had been through something like this, it was his leg that was broken, his dream that was crushed, and his life that was permanently changed. In a sad, ironic twist of fate, the same thing had happened to his only son. It just didn't seem fair.

I barely slept in the hospital that night, my leg wrapped in a giant cast and my heart broken. My teammates came to visit me, but it was hard for them to cheer me up. I stared out the window at a newly fallen snow and waited for the sun to rise. When it did, I met another doctor, who told me that I would have to wear the cast for three months before beginning my long recovery process. He warned me that my leg might never be the same again.

As I lay down in the hospital bed the next night, I couldn't help but replay that collision over and over again in my head. Why didn't I move out of the way? Why did I even go after that puck? Why was I kicking it? There were no answers to these questions, just the silence of a sad kid in a dark hospital room with a broken leg—and a broken dream.

CHAPTER EIGHT

A LONG ROAD

Skating toward the goal with the puck on the end of my stick, I am about to meet face to face with an NHL goalie for the first time. George Olen is one of the best in the business, and sneaking one past him is going to be tough. When I skate to about fifteen feet from him I start to make my move. First, I shift the puck over to my front side, faking a quick slap shot. Olen flinches, and I can see that I have an opening on his right. I quickly switch the puck over to my backhand and try to flick one up in the air, attempting to dump it over his right shoulder.

I am five feet away from him when the puck leaves my stick. I have spent so much time working on my backhand that I am very confident with it. As usual, the shot is on line and quite hard—nearly perfect—and it's heading toward the upper left-hand corner of the goal.

As the puck soars toward the goal, I wait for the flashing red light to illuminate above the goal. Just as I am about to pump my fist and begin celebrating my first NHL goal, Olen contorts his body so that his shoulder rises high in the air. I'm not even sure how he gets there, but somehow, the puck nicks the top of his shoulder and ricochets over the top of the goal.

Trying not to look disappointed, or surprised, I quickly skate to the back of the goal in an effort to get to the loose puck. But by the time I arrive, a Chicago defender is there to meet me. He punishes me with a big hit that nearly drops me. In the meantime, he grabs the puck and begins a fast break. I chase close behind him, eventually catching up to him at center ice. Rather than trying for the steal, I settle back into a good position to defend.

With just thirty seconds left on the Firestorm power play, I know that the four of us Elk players still on the ice are going to need to make one last stand. Sure enough, the Firestorm spread themselves out in our zone. They begin passing the puck around with great velocity. I have just gotten back into position at this point and am struggling to catch my breath.

Suddenly and without warning, their center makes a furious run toward the goal. Skating past our left wing, he is hit in stride by a perfect pass from his teammate, who stands a few feet in front of me. I extend my stick to stop the puck from getting to the middle of the ice, but it's just beyond my reach. A moment later, their center rears back and one-times a laser right at our goal.

With the crowd on their feet, our goalie, Dave Furion, makes an incredible kick save. The moment the puck leaves the stick of our opponent, Furion extends his legs into a full split. He looks like a gymnast as he touches his left leg to the post and stops the shot cold. He falls on top of the puck, then stands up, smacking it along the boards and back into Chicago's territory. The crowd erupts in applause!

By the time the puck crosses over the second blue line, the penalty is over and John Simpson leaps up from the box to join us on the ice. We've killed the penalty. Completely exhausted, I skate over to the bench for a line change. A few of my teammates slap my helmet, a sign of respect, as I grab for some water and spray it into my mouth.

Forty-eight hours after breaking my leg, I left North Memorial Medical Center wearing a giant cast. It was early November, and winter was just around the corner. I spoke to my doctor, Dr. Davis, for an hour before leaving the hospital. Among other things, he told me that my cast would likely come off in February. At that point I could *begin* my rehabilitation. I let him know that I was anxious to get that process started. The way I figured it, if I could get back to 100 percent by next August, which was nine months away, I could still try to walk onto a college hockey team next fall. Knowing he was a local, and a hockey fan who had been following my career, I confessed my goal to him.

Although he was supportive, the doctor was also very up front with me about the seriousness of my break. I had broken my femur, which is the largest bone in the human body. It is also a bone that takes time to heal properly—lots of time. The doctor warned me that even after my cast was removed, it would be a while before I would even be able to walk again. In terms of regaining the strength and agility I'd had before the injury—there was no timetable. He was quick to let me know that many people who break their femur are never the same afterwards. I could tell that he got no joy from it, but he fully prepared me for the possibility that I would never play hockey again.

Despite the seriousness of my injury, I tried to remain upbeat. It was hard, though. The pain in my leg was sharp, constant, and seemed to stretch from the tips of my toes up to my hip. Honestly, though, the pain in my heart was twice as bad.

I stayed home from school the next few days to rest my leg. I mostly lay around on the couch and watched television. Being a hockey player and a student, I'd never had so much time on my hands. Now that I did, I really didn't know what to do with it. It was pretty depressing. I read a few inspirational books about great athletes who overcame obstacles in achieving success, but nothing really cheered me up. By the time Monday came around, I was excited to go back to school and begin my life again.

The first day back was strange. All day long, kids, and teachers, too, came up to me to tell me how sorry they were. Their sympathy actually made me feel worse. I knew that my broken leg was bad news, but from the looks on their faces, you would have thought that someone had died. Every time somebody came up to me they had a similar facial expression—this expression seemed to be telling me that they felt bad for me because my hockey career was over. I just didn't see it that way, and although their sympathy was born of kindness, it was making me very upset.

Still, I forced myself to smile at them and I told each of them the same thing: "I'll be back out on the ice soon enough."

Some people didn't come up to me in the halls. Instead, they stared at me from a distance as I limped around on my crutches. I could hear them whispering as I passed by. Most of the stuff people were saying wasn't even true:

"The doctors said his leg will never be the same."

"You know, he could have been in the NHL."

"Minnesota College was going to offer him a scholarship. I heard there were NHL teams looking at him, too. Not anymore though."

"He broke it in three spots. I was at the game, it looked like his leg snapped in half—it was awful."

By the end of that day I wanted to crawl into a hole and hide. I was a senior in high school, just about to celebrate my eighteenth birthday, and all the plans I had been making since I was six years old had fallen to pieces. How would I ever make it to the NHL when I could barely make it to hockey practice without falling over?

Watching that first practice after my injury didn't feel real. I kept waiting for my leg to feel better so I could jump onto the ice and play. Sitting on the sidelines reminded me of my days as equipment manager in middle school. Just like back then, I desperately wanted to get into the game. It was different now, though. I was no longer feeling the pressure of trying to prove myself. I had already traveled down that road. That feeling was replaced by a sense of complete helplessness. There was nothing I could do to help my leg heal inside of that cast.

This feeling was intensified because I knew that with each passing day, my chances of playing in the NHL were diminishing. Hockey scholarships were being handed out to players all across the country. Not surprisingly, letters stopped coming my way. Just one year ago, there were hundreds of college scouts sending me brochures and invitations to come and visit their schools. By late

January, though, it had become quite clear that breaking my leg had ended my hopes for receiving a college hockey scholarship.

My cast came off on February 15, a full three months after my injury. The hockey season was over at this point, and most of the seniors I knew were making plans for college in the fall. In the morning on the day Dr. Davis was going to cut the cast off, I woke up whistling. It was going to be a great day. I felt as if my leg was about to be released from prison. I was sure that just seeing my leg would be a huge relief.

It only took about ten seconds for my cast to be cut and removed, but it took me much longer than that for the horrified expression on my face to lift. My leg was pale and skinny. I could barely move it and it smelled like something had died inside of that cast. Truth be told, I nearly threw up when I first breathed in. I had lost all muscle mass in the leg from being inactive for three months. I didn't even recognize this "thing" that the doctor insisted was my leg.

Getting down from the examination table was no easy task. I nearly fell to the ground as I put weight on my leg for the first time in months. I glanced down at my leg—totally confused—and poked it with my finger. The leg was still there, but it had absolutely no strength, and barely any feeling. The strange thing was that, other than being much skinnier, it looked pretty normal, and it didn't hurt—but it didn't work right either. With my mother by my side, a few tears welled up in my eyes. She looked over at me, and I swallowed hard to avoid crying. It was then that I realized just how high the mountain was that I was going to have to climb. I left the hospital still hobbling around on crutches. Cast or no cast, my leg was still in very bad shape.

I got a letter a few weeks later from Minnesota College that really cheered me up. No, they didn't ask me to play hockey for them—but I had been accepted to attend the college as a student for the fall semester. My academic record, not my hockey skills, had earned me a ticket to college. There was no scholarship offer, but I was going to have the opportunity to get a college education at a top university. The next day, I mailed in all the appropriate paperwork, letting them know that I accepted their offer and would be attending school in Minneapolis next fall.

Despite my limp left leg, I wasn't ready to give up on my hockey career yet. My plan, since I had been a kid, was to get a hockey scholarship to Minnesota College, play well there, and then get drafted by an NHL team. When I broke my leg, that plan fell apart. But I wasn't quitting yet. I was starting to understand what Dad had told me a long time ago: "Your dream only dies the day you let it die." I kept this thought in my head as I made new plans. I wasn't ready to let it die yet.

In a few months, I would attend Minnesota College's Men's Hockey Team open tryouts. There were two spots available for walk-ons and I planned on taking one of them. First, I needed to make a fast recovery before the August tryout.

My preparations began when I started working with a physical trainer five days a week. Every morning before school my alarm would ring at four thirty. I would leave my house at five o'clock to start my one-mile walk to the hospital. This was the program that my trainer suggested. I was supposed to walk slowly—never speeding up to a run. I did exactly what he told me. Every day my walk got a little easier.

When I arrived at the training facility, we would do stretches and strength-building exercises. My leg was improving, but everything was happening very slowly. Each time I looked at the calendar, I panicked, wondering if my leg would be strong enough for tryouts. We were creeping closer and closer to August 10, the date hockey tryouts would be held at Martin Arena—also known as "The Snake Pit." This was the home of the Minnesota College Silver Snakes, and it was the ice I had dreamed of skating on since I was a little boy. Before I could skate though, I had to learn how to walk, and then run, all over again.

I graduated from high school with honors at the end of June and celebrated with my friends and family. My final grade point average was a 3.7, which made me the fifteenth-ranked graduating senior. The next year, when I began college in Minneapolis, I planned to major in sports medicine. In rehabbing from my injury, I had become fascinated by the field of sports medicine. As I worked hard on my leg, I took mental notes on the different techniques my trainer used. For the first time in my life, there was something besides hockey that I was very interested in. Not that I was giving up on hockey yet.

By the end of June, I was riding a bicycle five miles a day and starting to feel like my leg was approaching full strength. It was hard to tell, though. I knew that I wouldn't know the extent of my recovery for sure until I got out there and tested it on the ice. Finally, on July 10, one month before hockey tryouts were to take place, my trainer gave me permission to begin athletic activities. I had made it all the way back! I no longer walked with a limp, and I often found myself forgetting that my leg had ever even been injured. It had been eight months since I was lying on that ice in pain, grasping my leg. During that time, I had worked as hard as I possibly could to get back to where I was before the injury. After teaching myself how to walk, and how to run again, there was one thing left to do: start playing hockey.

The following Saturday morning was an exciting day. The sun was shining and I was once again whistling through my shower. I planned to put on my skates and return to the ice for the first time! I still had the key to the middle school rink that Coach Nielson had let me use when I was the equipment manager. During high school, I would go down there all the time to practice. Once in a while, I would see Coach Nielson and we'd talk. But when I flicked on the lights and opened up the door to the locker room on that Saturday morning, nobody was there.

I put on my skates and made sure to tie the laces tightly, the way my father had always taught me. It felt great to put on those skates again. Next, I put on pads, to simulate the experience of playing in a real game. Then I went out onto the ice. It was really weird to be skating again. I took a slow lap around the rink, barely pumping my legs, just feeling out the ice. During that lap, I couldn't help but think about my leg constantly. I couldn't shake this feeling of fear. It weighed heavily on my mind, and I felt like I was skating with a piano on my back. I had never been so slow or scared on the ice before.

After warming up for a minute, I started to set up the cones the way I had several years ago. I dropped my lucky puck at the end of the cones and dragged out a single goal, the way Coach Nielson had done during middle school practice. Then I skated slowly back to the first cone. Before trying to run through the cones course, I stretched one last time. If I was going to try and make a comeback, I would need to be able to skate at full speed without pain. My trainer warned me that I should respect any pain that I felt and stop athletic activities immediately. There was no way to tell how far along I was in my recovery until I tested my leg at full speed. Ignoring any pain that I felt would almost certainly lead to me injuring my leg again. I kept this in mind as I started my run.

I began to skate. I went around the first cone slowly and smoothly and then started to pick up speed around the second. When I reached that cone, I really tried to turn on the jets, pumping my legs with everything I had. For a moment, I was flying through the cones course the way I used to. And in the next moment, I was stopping abruptly with a sharp pain in my leg. It happened that fast.

I took a second to stretch out my leg, assuming that the pain I felt was just some rust. Then I skated slowly back to the beginning of the cones course and started again. Sure enough, when I reached top speed, I felt that pain again, only this time, it was worse. I stopped skating immediately, flicked off my helmet in frustration, and slammed my stick to the ground.

My body simply wasn't able to keep up with my will. I wasn't anywhere close to where I needed to be if I wanted to make a college hockey team. I needed more time to strengthen my leg. But I didn't have time. The tryouts were in three weeks! Who was I kidding? If I couldn't get through these cones without pain, then I wasn't even close to ready. Plus, I wasn't as fast as I used to be. Without my speed, I was just another hockey player—and at five feet six inches tall, I was too small not to be quick. Everything seemed hopeless at that point. I just wasn't the same player anymore. I had lost it.

I dropped to my knees and started to cry. My sobs echoed throughout the empty arena, and my tears melted into the ice when they hit it. I sat like that for about fifteen minutes, then I put the goal and the cones back in the equipment locker, shut off the lights, and left. I was completely devastated. All the hard work I had put in to rehab my leg was pointless. I was never going to play hockey again.

I drove around Robbinsdale for an hour or two before heading home. When I walked through the door with tears in my eyes, I saw Dad standing there. I looked him right in the face as I said, "I'm ready to quit now."

CHAPTER NINE

COMEBACK

*The third period begins with the game still scoreless.
For the hockey purists in the stands, this game is shaping up to
be a classic: two teams playing great defense, and two
goaltenders refusing to let up. In Minnesota, the crowds are
knowledgeable and they really appreciate good hockey. For
the casual fan, scoring and big checks are the most exciting
parts of the game. But a true hockey fan can appreciate the
game's subtleties.*

*Dad used to tell me that scoreless games tended to bring
out the best in players because every moment was so critical.
Despite playing evenly for sixty minutes, the game could be
won or lost with one great shot or pass—and just as easily with
one player's lapse in concentration. Tonight, as the clock ticks
down during a scoreless tie, the players on the ice shift mental
and emotional gears. The game becomes frantic and reaches a
completely different level of intensity.*

With eight minutes remaining in the final period, I can feel this change take place. It's in the air and the crowd picks up on it as well, rising to their feet. The pace quickens, the hits are harder than ever, and the shots on goal are more frequent. The excitement is palpable.

I am well rested, after sitting on the bench for the last ten minutes of the second period. I watch from the sidelines as the battle continues. After an offside call on the Firestorm's center, we win the face-off. We now have possession with eight minutes remaining in the game. Spreading out on offense, we pass the puck around the perimeter. Our hope is that a Firestorm defender will get overeager, allowing us to make a run at the goal, and perhaps get off a clean shot.

We have no such luck. In fact, the opposite happens. Impatient to score, John Simpson launches a long slap shot from the blue line. It sails wide of the net, and the Firestorm recover the puck. They begin a three-on-two break. Their center fakes a pass to his right wing, but instead of giving up the puck, he cuts back toward the middle of the ice, passing at the last moment to his left. The puck reaches a forward about ten feet from the goal. He unleashes a one-timer—meaning that he shoots the puck off of the pass, without controlling it first.

Dave Furion never sees this laser coming. He dives left at the last second, but he fails to reach the puck. The sound of the black disc clanking against the left post is a welcomed one. The shot just missed. One inch to the right, and it would have been a goal. Instead, Dave leaps on top of the loose puck and the whistle blows, stopping play.

We are about to face off again, this time in a dangerous

spot in our zone. Coach Lewis looks down the bench, and calls me into the game. I jump to my feet—surprised that I am being called in at such a critical point. I line up on the right wing, waiting for the chance to get my stick on the puck and break up the ice. There are about six minutes remaining at this point. The crowd is screaming, and banging their feet on the floor of Elk Arena. The building is literally shaking.

The puck drops and we win the face-off. Immediately, I am off down the right side, showing a burst of speed that no one is able to match. The puck comes my way, but just as I am about to receive it, I am checked. Although I stay on my feet, I lose sight of the puck, and the fast break chance is over.

The day after I felt that shooting pain, I hung up my skates. When I left the ice, I had officially given up on my dream. It took a while before I was able to come to grips with my decision to quit the sport I had grown up playing. Although I wanted to continue fighting against the odds, my leg wouldn't cooperate. The fact was: I simply wasn't the same hockey player. This was a hard truth to come to terms with.

I decided that I had worked too hard during these last ten years to embarrass myself at a college hockey tryout, trying to skate on one leg against some of the top athletes in the nation. Without being 100 percent, the chances of me making the team were slim to none. Plus, there was the risk of re-injury. Judging by how bad the pain was in my leg after skating for just a few minutes, I was sure that skating for a few hours would do me in.

Three weeks after my comeback attempt at the middle school rink, I packed almost everything I owned into ten big cardboard boxes, threw them in the back of Dad's pick-up truck, and headed off to college.

Despite not playing hockey, my freshman year of college was great. I didn't focus on the past. Instead, I looked toward a bright future. During that first month of school, I had so much fun and met lots of new friends. I even met a girl. Rachel Parker was her name, and although we had only hung out a few times, she was definitely girlfriend material. Living away from home was a big adjustment for me. Doing my own laundry, living with a roommate, and not eating homemade meals at night was a huge change. I got used to it, but I don't think I'd ever realized how much my parents did for me until I was on my own.

By the time hockey season started, I was fully adjusted to school. I knew my way around campus, was acing my classes, and was continuing to rehabilitate my leg. Like I said, my hockey dreams were over, but that didn't mean I had stopped trying to get my leg back to 100 percent. I continued to work hard at the gym every day, and I rode my bike around campus everywhere I went. Majoring in sports medicine certainly made me more interested in my own injury. It also made me focus on my rehab twice as hard. Not only was I getting better, but through my injury, I was learning a lot.

I followed the hockey team very closely, attending all of their home games and a few of their practices as well. Because of my sports medicine major, I even got to help the trainers treat a few of their minor injuries in the training room. They were a talented bunch and seemed like nice guys as well.

At the end of one practice, I bumped into the assistant coach, Pete Mitchum. He was the same guy who had sent me that recruiting letter during my junior year of high school. He remembered me and my injury, and let me know that he was real sorry the way things had turned out for me. It was a short conversation, but it got me thinking thoughts that I knew I shouldn't have been thinking about: *Sure, this team is really good. But they're thin at forward—having me on that right wing would make them better.*

Thoughts like these took me nowhere in a hurry. I would end up spending the next few hours replaying my injury in my head again and again. What-if scenarios like these always left me wondering about what life would have been like if I would have just moved to my left a few feet during that collision. These questions often kept me awake at night. I tried hard not to let them creep into my conscience. During conversations with my father, a man who knew about these thoughts all too well, I learned that the best way to deal with my injury was to focus on the future. So that's what I tried to do.

When I wasn't thinking about hockey during those first few months, I was riding my bike. Every day, I would pedal from my dorm room to class, which was about a fifteen-minute ride—and then back again. My leg was starting to feel much better at this point, and from what I knew about rehabilitation, both from my experiences and from class, exercise was a good thing. I didn't feel any real pain in my leg any longer, which was great. Part of me wanted to push it, and find out what my limits were on this "new" leg. The other part of me was scared to death of another injury. This constant battle within my own head was unresolved. Although contradicting thoughts like these ultimately kept me away from the ice, they also drew me to it.

My dormitory was on the top of a really steep hill. So,

when I left my room in the morning for my ride to class, I would walk my bike down it, fearing that going too fast would cause another injury. On the way home, I would walk the bike back up the hill. Although ascending the hill was good exercise for my leg, it was also a constant reminder of my injury. To be honest, it was difficult to see people from my dorm racing each other on their bikes and skateboards, up and down that hill. I was a competitive person by nature, so watching them without participating was hard for me. But every time I was about to try it myself—whether it was down the hill in the morning, or back up the hill in the afternoon—the fear took hold of me. I would hop off my bike, and start walking.

By early March, my freshman year was close to over. I was sitting in the dining hall having lunch with my roommate Jeff, when we started to talk about hockey. It was a subject I rarely got into these days. Today was different, though. The Silver Snakes had qualified for the NCAA tournament, and Jeff was discussing their first-round match-up against Michigan State College. The game was going to be taking place the next day, so everybody on campus was talking about it.

One thing led to another and soon we were discussing the intramural hockey league that Jeff had recently signed up for. The first game of their new season also started the next day. Jeff had gotten a team together, and although he had asked me to join the week before, I had declined. Now he was practically begging me, because they needed another player. "You played hockey in high school, right, Wayne?"

"Yeah," I said, barely looking up from my lunch.

"Were you any good?" he asked. "I mean, for a little guy,"

he joked.

I smiled. "I was pretty good—for a little guy, that is." Then I got serious for a second, "but you know, I hurt my leg. I don't play any more."

"I know all about your leg." Jeff started to imitate my voice in a joking way. "I can't play flag football—my leg. I can't go running with you guys—my leg. I know all about your leg, Wayne! The funny thing is, your leg is fine! You ride your bike ten miles a day. I can't even ride two miles, and my leg is in perfect health! Besides, I never see you icing it or anything. It never even seems to bother you."

I tried to fake a laugh, but really I was pretty surprised by what he was saying. I hadn't realized how much I'd let my injured leg affect my life until now.

Jeff continued, "I don't think it would kill you to skate around for a little bit. Besides, it's just for fun, and if your leg starts to hurt, you can sit out. We've got subs."

I thought about this for a second. Beneath the table I shook my leg. I even touched it with my right hand. The truth was, Jeff was right. The leg felt great. It had felt great for a month or two now. I just hadn't really been able to admit that to myself. Although the improvements were good news, acknowledging that my leg was okay was like saying that there was no reason for me not to be going after my dream again. I mean, what was stopping me? In the last few weeks, since I had begun to realize the extent to which my leg had healed, this thought, more than any other, was keeping me awake at night.

Jeff looked over at me. I was lost, deep in thought. "Hello—anybody home?"

Before I even realized what I was doing, my lips moved, and two words popped out of my mouth. "I'll play."

I guess the thought of playing hockey the next morning was just too much for me to pass up. I could not deny myself the chance to play the sport I loved. Besides, just because I wasn't going to play in the NHL didn't mean that I couldn't play hockey for fun. I thought about my father—he didn't make it to the NHL, but even with his bum leg, he played the game whenever he could. So I caved in, burying the fear of getting injured in the back of my head.

Twenty minutes later, I arrived at the bottom of the big hill below my dorm. Like I always did, I hopped off my bike and started to walk up the hill. Then I stopped myself. I walked the bike back down to the base of the hill and hopped back on it. *I can do this,* I thought. Staring up at the top of the hill, I started to pedal. In a few seconds, I was peddling fast and hard, climbing the hill quickly. There were a few other people making their way up the steepest hill on the entire campus. I passed by them like they were standing still.

As I pumped my legs and crept closer and closer to the top, a huge smile swept across my face. I felt no pain in my leg—none. When I reached the front door to my dorm, instead of grabbing my bike and carrying it up to my room, I raced back down the hill again. People must have thought I had gone crazy. Once I reached the bottom, I turned around and climbed back to the top again—this time, faster than before. My leg felt great! There was no pain or soreness whatsoever.

That night, I slept soundly.

The next morning was Saturday, and I was supposed to meet Jeff and his friends at the rink at noon. I was so excited just to step on the ice again. Plus, I was anxious to test my leg out off of the bike. After all, I hadn't skated since late July, just eight months after my injury. That was the day I had officially ended my hockey career.

I laced up my skates and threw on the pads we were using for the intramural game, along with a plain yellow jersey. As always, I took my time lacing up my skates. Feeling the hard leather against my ankles made me happy.

When I got out onto the ice, as usual, I was the smallest one there. I started warming up by skating around in a circle. I moved slowly around the rink at first, adjusting to the feel of the ice again. I have to say, it felt great to be out there. Then I started to pick up some speed, testing my leg. By the time I reached top speed, I noticed that every person in the small rink was staring at me. I was flying. Every bit of speed that I once had was back—and then some. The look on my face was probably similar to the wide-eyed, gape-mouthed faces of the people witnessing my speed-skating display. Total shock!

All the rehabilitation work I had done on my legs had made them stronger than ever. I couldn't believe how fast I was skating! The best news, though, was that I felt absolutely no pain. My recovery seemed to be complete. It was as if my leg had never been broken in the first place.

I came to a stop near center ice, spraying snow high into the air. It was then that I noticed Jeff and a few other guys who were wearing yellow jerseys. They were staring at me in awe. Jeff skated a bit awkwardly up to me. "Are you kidding me, Wayne?" he asked. "I've never seen anyone skate like that in my life—and I'm a season ticket holder for the Elk!" He laughed. "You're like, the fastest guy in the world!"

I smiled. "That was always my plan. I bet there's somebody faster, though," I said, completely serious.

Jeff looked like he had just seen a ghost when he said, "Whatever position you play, you're starting."

That game was really fun. It was kind of unfair, because most of the guys I was playing against weren't really hockey players. They were just out for a good time on a Saturday afternoon. A few of them had played some high school hockey, and one or two of them were decent. For the most part, though, they were amateurs. They got more than they bargained for on that Saturday. I was every bit the same player I had been during my junior season. The only difference was, I was faster and stronger. Sure, I was a bit rusty, but I found that when I had the puck, I could skate around any defender and take a shot on goal whenever I felt like it. The strength in my legs was amazing!

After I scored five or six times, I stopped shooting. The last thing I wanted to do was take the fun out of it for everyone else. I sat on the sidelines during the last few minutes and stared at my leg. *Was this really happening?* I wondered.

When we finished that game, Jeff and I went out for a burger. We sat in a booth with a view of the television. The NCAA tournament was on, and we didn't want to miss the Snakes' first game. I felt so happy—the happiest I had been since I hurt my leg. To my total surprise, I was still a great player. When I injured my leg and was unable to rehab in time for last summer's tryout, I lost my confidence. After climbing that hill on my bike, and then the display I put on when I hit the ice, I was slowly getting it back.

With his mouth stuffed, Jeff spoke to me while we both

stared at the big screen television. He pointed to the game. "You should be playing with those guys. You're unbelievable, Wayne."

"Thanks," I said, only half listening.

Jeff looked away from the television and then right at me. "I'm serious, man. You should go out for the team next year. You'll make it."

When Jeff spoke those words, my heart started to race. I shrugged my shoulders at his comment, but the truth was, I was thinking the exact same thing. Without realizing it, I reached down and touched my leg. Appropriately, I was watching the Snakes play in the NCAA tournament as we had this conversation. This was the biggest stage in collegiate hockey. I wished that I was playing too.

Maybe Jeff was right. There was no physical reason for me not to try out next year. The only problem was that it had taken me all this time just to come to grips with the fact that I wasn't going to be a professional hockey player. I was studying sports medicine, and I really liked it. I had a girl I liked, some good friends—everything was going great for me. I just didn't know if my heart could take being broken again by hockey. *What if I tried out and didn't make it?* I wondered. *What if I hurt my leg again?*

I voiced these doubts to Jeff: "You know, I used to dream about playing in the NHL every day. I practiced hard, and I was good. Then I got hurt and—" I trailed off. A moment later, I finished my thought. "When that dream died, a piece of me died. I don't know if I can go through that again. Besides," I said, "have you ever heard of a five-foot-six sophomore walking onto one of the best college hockey programs in the world?"

"No," he confessed, as he took a giant bite of his burger. "But I've also never heard of a five-foot-six sophomore skating like you do. You were awesome out there today. Unstoppable!" As Jeff spoke the last syllable of this word, a piece of burger flew out of his mouth.

"That's gross!" I laughed, breaking the tension I was feeling. "The guys playing on TV up there," I pointed to the big screen, "they're about a million times better than the guys we played against today. You know that, right?"

It was then that Jeff said something that I'll never forget. "I used to be a great speller when I was a kid. Did I ever tell you that?" I had no idea what he was talking about.

"What?" I asked.

"When I was a kid, I entered all these spelling bees. I practiced all the time, too. I actually won for the whole state of Minnesota one year. I was kind of a natural."

"No kidding," I said, not knowing what he was talking about and why he had just brought this up.

"Anyway," he went on, "there was this big spelling bee at the end of the year during eighth grade—it was a national thing. The winners from each state were supposed to sign up for a chance to win a college scholarship."

"Cool. So, did you get the scholarship?" I asked.

"No," he said, taking a bite of his burger. "I didn't bother signing up for the contest."

"Why not?" I asked.

"I figured, I'm good, but I'm not *that* good. So I sat home and watched the competition on television." Then he paused, looking right into my eyes. "You know, I didn't spell one word wrong during that entire competition. Not one. When I clicked the television off, I just started crying. I cried because of what could have happened if I would have tried." He paused, looking up at the television set and then back at me. "As funny as it sounds, that was my dream at the time, and I didn't go for it. My point is, if you've got a shot at this thing, you have to try. You don't want to end up watching these guys for the rest of your life thinking 'that should have been me.'"

Jeff's story was exactly what I needed to here. Before he even finished talking, I knew what I had to do. "You're right, man." I said. Then, with my burger still sitting on the table, half-eaten, I jumped up from the table. "I've gotta go, bro." I dropped a twenty dollar bill onto the table, and ran out. "Thanks!" I yelled back to him.

I heard Jeff calling "Where are you going?" as I flew out the door. I hopped on my bike and started pedaling as fast as I could. I had to get to a hockey rink. I had a lot of work to do.

CHAPTER TEN

HOCKEY DREAMS

After deciding to make my comeback, I played a ton of hockey over the next four months. And, even though the competition wasn't great, I continued with Jeff and his friends in the intramural league. I also played in a local men's league on Tuesday nights in downtown Minneapolis. The players there were much better, and I got some really good practice in. I even took some hard hits, which helped me develop confidence in my bad leg. Each time I got hit, I would smile big when I got back up again. I was starting to feel more and more secure in the fact that my leg was fully healed. By the time the summer rolled around, I barely thought about my injury while I played.

Dad was my biggest cheerleader. I think that coming back from my injury was even more exciting for him than it was for me. I can't really explain it, except to say that maybe I was righting the wrong in his life. His injury had been so severe that it ended his hockey career before it even started. He confessed that when I got hurt, he often stayed up at night, wondering if our family had some kind of curse on it or something. When I made my comeback, he realized that it was just the opposite—we were very lucky.

Every time we talked while I was away, he would remind me that the best way to get myself ready for the tryout in August was to skate, pass, and shoot until I could barely stand. "You came this far, Wayne—the road was long, and you hit some big bumps along the way. But you're still standing. I really admire you for that." His words were inspirational. Every time I wanted to stop skating to go home and rest, I would hear him again. His voice and those words helped drive me toward accomplishing my goals.

I came home to Robbinsdale on May 15. I spent some time with Ricky and some of my friends from high school who I hadn't seen since Thanksgiving break. Ricky was playing on the basketball team for Southern Ohio College. At six-foot nine-inches tall, Ricky had grown another two inches since high school. His giant frame standing next to mine was a strange sight.

After Ricky and I took a ride around town, we went down to the arcade at the mall. It was kind of weird being back at the local hangout, but not really being local. We both felt it, too—it was as if we had outgrown it or something. Mom used to tell me that life had a funny way of talking to you sometimes. When we stepped into that arcade, I heard life telling me that I was getting old.

We walked over to the pop-a-shot machine and put in a couple of quarters. I was terrible, but ironically, Ricky the basketball star was even worse. "One year of Division I basketball under your belt, and now you stink at pop-a-shot." I laughed. "What happened to you? You used to be the master."

Ricky laughed. "I promise, my shot has improved—on a

ten-foot rim, though."

I looked up at him and laughed, "If I was as tall as Godzilla, I would have a pretty good shot too. You're basically eye-to-eye with the hoop, Ricky. How hard can it be to put it in?"

"And you're so close to the ice, I'm surprised you don't freeze to it." Ricky pushed me jokingly. "Now pipe down, shrimp, or I'll squash you with my size sixteen's." He lifted his leg, showing off a foot that was literally bigger than half of my torso. It was great hanging out with Scared Stiff Rick again. As much as things had changed, they had stayed the same.

We grabbed a bite to eat, and Ricky told me all about his experiences riding the bench for a season at Southern Ohio. He played a total of eighteen minutes that year. Although it was frustrating for him, he said that he'd learned a lot and was looking forward to next season. I was happy for him. We talked about my return to hockey, and Ricky told me that he "knew I'd be back on the ice all along." I guess that, deep down, I knew it too.

With tryouts a few months away, I didn't spend too much time with friends that summer. Instead, I got down to business quickly. I started heading down to Mickey's Ice Arena every night, playing in scrimmage games and in several leagues as well. Dad came with me a few times, but he was getting too old to play for too long. (I didn't tell him that, though.)

By the middle of June, I was playing the best hockey I'd ever played. Being a few years older, I was much stronger than during my high school days. Sure, I was still small, but I was compact and muscular. My balance had improved by leaps and bounds, and I could absorb a check with the best of them. This was because of all the rehab work I had done on my legs—they were like tree trunks—holding up a very small tree. In terms of speed, I was unmatched anywhere I laced up my skates. Every time I touched the puck, all the players on the opposing team would skate as fast as they could toward their own zone. They were scared of me, and it felt great. I tried not to get a big head out there, knowing that the players I would be playing alongside at the tryout would be much better than the guys back home.

I went back to school a couple of days before the tryouts. Once I got there, I unpacked my stuff and tried to rest for a day or two before the big day. When I arrived at The Snake Pit on the first morning of the two-day tryout, I bumped into Pete Mitchum again—the assistant coach who had recruited me during my junior high school season.

He walked right up to me and shook my hand. "How's it going, Wayne?" He paused, "Are you here to watch the tryout?"

"No, sir." I said, "I'm here to try out myself."

Coach Mitchum looked a bit confused. "What about your leg?" he asked.

"It feels great, Coach. I've been working hard rehabbing it for about eighteen months now. I'm hoping you guys have a spot for me." I said, flushing red in the face as I spoke.

"Well, if you can play the way you did in high school we might."

In the middle of this conversation, some of the other guys who were attending the tryout started to pour in. He ended our conversation abruptly. "I'll see you out there," he said, patting me on the back.

I played amazing hockey on that first day. Scrimmaging against the first line, guys who were all on scholarship, I showed that I could hang. In fact, I scored twice and played suffocating defense. I also proved myself to be the fastest guy on the ice—which I'm sure surprised Coach Mitchum. I was hoping that my speed, and ability to stay on the ice for a long period of time without tiring, proved that my leg was 100 percent healthy.

Of course, I was still the smallest guy on the ice, but I wasn't playing like it. Two years away from the game had left a fire burning in my belly. Every time I got the chance, I used my powerful legs to push me forward, laying out an opponent with a body check. When they tried to return the favor, they found it impossible to get a clean hit on me. I was simply too fast, too elusive, and too small.

The second day of tryouts was just as good as the first. This time, I noticed Coach Mitchum looking over at me while he was talking to the head coach, Jim Morton. Coach Morton was nodding his head and taking notes. The way I had played during those two days, led me to believe that I would earn a spot on the team. I just hoped I wasn't about to be disappointed again.

Lying in bed that night, I tossed and turned, chewing at my fingernails. This was my last chance, and I knew it. If I didn't get a phone call tomorrow morning, which was when Coach Mitchum said he would make the calls for the walk-ons, my hockey career was over—again. With the cordless phone resting on my chest, I finally fell asleep a few hours later.

At eight thirty in the morning on August 12, I was awoken by the ring of the phone. Still half-asleep when I picked it up, I quickly jumped out of bed when I heard the voice on the other end of the line. It was Coach Mitchum, letting me know that I was now one of two new members of the Silver Snakes men's hockey team. I couldn't have been more excited. I must have thanked him ten times. My dream was back on track!

That sophomore season was great. I played on the second line and adjusted pretty quickly to the college game. Unlike when I joined the middle school team, the guys were great, even if they did begin referring to me as Little Wayne. The nickname had bothered me when I was a kid, but now I found that I was beginning to like it. When people called me Little Wayne it reminded me of how hard I had fought to get here, overcoming my size, and my injury.

Being a student-athlete made keeping my grades up a little more difficult, but I adjusted. I maintained a high average, and never missed a hockey meeting, lifting session, practice, or game. We had a good season, making it to the NCAA tournament as the number two seeded team. Unfortunately, we were knocked out in the second round. For most schools, this would have been considered a banner year—but we had much higher expectations at Minnesota College. We expected to win the national title every season. Anything less was disappointing.

I turned twenty-one during my junior season and was starting to feel more and more grown up. Many guys my age were forego-ing their last two years of college to play in the NHL, but I knew that my dreams had to wait until I finished getting my education. Sure, if and when I made it to the NHL, I would end up a twenty-two-year old rookie. By NHL standards, that was a little old, but I didn't care. I was going to finish what I had started and get my diploma.

After contributing during my sophomore year, Coach Morton offered me a full scholarship for the rest of my time as a Snake. This made my decision to stay in school even easier. Mom and Dad were very excited about this because now my tuition was free. As I signed the scholarship papers, I promised Coach Morton that I wouldn't let him down.

I played great hockey that season, leading our team in assists and goals. I was a fan favorite, too. Mom said that people loved to root for the underdog, and she was right. I was definitely the underdog out there. By mid-season, every time I touched the puck the crowd would scream "Lit-tle Wayne, Lit-tle Wayne," picking up on the nickname my teammates had given me. It was pretty cool to be recognized by the crowd, and it definitely got me fired up to play my best.

What was happening with our team was even more exciting than my personal successes. We were playing amazing hockey. After our first twelve games, the Silver Snakes were still undefeated. Although we lost unlucky game number thirteen, we never lost again that year. Not even in the NCAA tournament, where we swept away the competition to win a national title.

My senior year didn't result in a back-to-back national championship, but it was still a great year. I began to stand out as a top player and was even picked on the All-Conference team. Being recognized as one of the top players in the conference was something I was very proud of. It was also an excellent way to get the NHL talent scouts to take me, and my five foot six inch frame, seriously.

When that season ended, so did my college career. It had been five years since my leg injury and I felt no residual effects. I finished up school that May, once again, graduating with honors. I had a degree in sports medicine, and planned on pursuing that field if my hockey career didn't work out.

On the day of the NHL draft, I waited at home to see where I would be selected. I was pleasantly surprised when I was chosen seventeenth in the second round. What really excited me, though, was the team that selected me. I must have been the luckiest guy in the world. Beginning in a few months, I was going to be suiting up for the Minnesota Elk, the team I had been cheering for my entire life. I couldn't have asked for anything more.

This leads me back to where I am right now: standing on the ice, dazed after getting checked hard with just over five minutes remaining in a scoreless tie against the rival Chicago Firestorm. They regain possession of the puck, and I settle back on defense, drifting into position on the right side.

Before I even know what has happened, a hard slap shot is saved into the glove of Dave Furion. That puck was moving so quickly that I never even saw it. He passes it out to Alexi Kornikov, who slows things down and waits for the rest of us to get set. We are ready to begin our attack. With less than four minutes remaining now, we are well aware that this may be our final attack before the game is forced into overtime.

Alexi passes it over to me on the right side. I skate forward with a short burst, before stopping in front of an eager defender. I play with the puck for a second, making sure to keep it clear of him. Then, from the corner of my eye, I can see that Alexi is making a run toward the goal. I skate forward a bit, drawing the defender just close enough so that a passing lane opens up for me to sneak the puck through. My plan works perfectly. The defender approaches me, and I slide a pass just past his stick as he lays a punishing blow that nearly knocks me over.

The puck is about to reach Alexi, who is hovering just in front of the goal, but it is deflected at the last second, ricocheting off a second defender's skate. The puck is now loose, and a few players are scrambling for it right in front of Chicago's goal. It is a messy scrum with bodies flying onto the ice and sticks smacking against one another. I move in a little closer, but not too close—I am sure to stay far enough back to defend against a possible fast break.

In the chaos, the puck shoots out toward me. I am too far out to accurately one-time a shot on goal. Still, I know that the defense is expecting this rushed reaction from a rookie like myself. I try to use my knowledge of hockey to my advantage. As the puck sails toward me, I rear back, as if I am about to take a big swing at the puck. I can already see the goalie staring at me. He is prepared to react to my shot. As the puck gets closer, I slow my swing, stopping it just before I make contact with the puck. This gets rid of the defender in front of me, as he drops to his knees to stop my shot—but there is no shot.

With him on the ice near the right side of the goal, I skate in closer, angling myself around the pile of players in the middle of the ice. The closer I get to the goal, the more players start to skate toward me. Moving to my left, around a second fallen defender, I can see a small opening in the top left corner of the goal. Without thinking, I reach back and fire a shot that looks to be on line.

Somehow, though, it is saved! My second shot of the game—and the second amazing save by the goalie. I can't *believe it!*

The puck glances off the goalies left leg, which he somehow extended over his head to guard the top left post. It flops around in front of the goal. Somebody gets their stick on it—I can't really tell if it is us or them—but the puck gets loose again. I can see it to the left of the goal, spinning like a top. I charge it.

I am about to shoot again, when I notice Alexi Kornikov standing unguarded on the right side of the goal. I don't dare turn my head in his direction, which would be a clear signal to the goalie, basically inviting him to change his position. Instead, I lock my eyes on a spot in the back of the net and pretend to take a big slap shot. I rear my stick back, but rather than firing a shot, I flick a quick pass across the front of the goal, just around the goalie's oversized stick. Alexi hits a one timer into the empty net for a goal.

The entire arena erupts! They literally explode! The red light above the goal goes off, and the horn sounds. My heart feels like it is about to jump out of my jersey and dance. Alexi Kornikov skates over to me and grabs me, "Great pass, kid! You feisty and good!" he screams.

I raise my fist in the air and pump it. Then I look over at Coach, who is subbing in a fresh line to finish the game with just three minutes left. As I skate to the bench to grab a bottle of water, I can hear the crowd chanting. "Lit-tle Wayne, Lit-tle Wayne." The fans in Minnesota know me well. My parents are in the stands cheering. Mom is crying, and I nearly lose it just looking at her. For the next three minutes the crowd stays on their feet, chanting "Lit-tle Wayne, Lit-tle Wayne" until the final horn sounds and the game is over.

When I glance at the glowing numbers on the scoreboard and see Minnesota Elk 1, Chicago Firestorm 0, I have to smile. I'm really here—I've made it. It's an awesome moment. All of my hockey dreams are coming true.

TEST YOURSELF...ARE YOU A PROFESSIONAL READER?

<u>Chapter 1: New Skates</u>

Describe Wayne's first pair of skates.

Which famous hockey player is Wayne named after?

What is the name of the ice rink that Wayne skates on for the first time?

<u>ESSAY</u>

Think of something that you love to do. In an essay, describe the first time you ever participated in this activity. How did this new activity make you feel? Why do you think trying something new is so exciting?

<u>Chapter 2: Little Wayne</u>

Wayne brings his English book with him to Science class. Why did he mix up the two books?

What was Wayne's nickname? Do you think he liked that nickname? Why or why not?

What did Wayne do once he realized that he was "past the point of no return"?

ESSAY

Wayne gets picked on by a few of the eighth grade boys in this chapter. What did you think about the way Wayne handled being picked on? How could he have handled the situation better? What would you have done?

Chapter 3: Tryouts

How much had Wayne grown during the past year? How does Wayne measure himself?

What excuse did Ricky make up so that he wouldn't have to go to hockey tryouts? What was his real reason for not trying out?

According to Coach Nielson, why didn't Wayne make the team?

ESSAY

At the end of this chapter, Wayne says, "My big mouth had cost me big this time. It cost me a spot on the team." What does this mean? Think of a time in your life when your "big mouth" affected you negatively. Describe what happened.

Chapter 4: The Equipment Manager

In this chapter, Wayne steps onto the ice for the first time as a member of the Minnesota Elk. Which team is he playing against to open the season?

Name three jobs which Wayne was responsible for as the equipment manager.

What were some of the "little hockey details" that Wayne started to write about in his notebook?

ESSAY

In this chapter, Wayne's father says, "Your dream only dies the day you let it die." What does this quote mean? Do you think this is always true? Why or why not?

Chapter 5: Big Break

How did Wayne's flu shot save his season?

What caused Wayne to fall during his run through the cones course?

What position did Wayne play the first time he stepped onto the ice against Plymouth?

ESSAY

In this chapter Wayne is very excited to play hockey again. When he first steps onto the ice, he is over-excited and doesn't play his best. Coach Nielson tells Wayne to "let the game come to you." What do you think this means? Why can trying too hard mess you up sometimes?

Chapter 6: Teammates

Who ended up being one of Wayne's closest friends on the team? Why was this surprising?

Why did the team play worse when Darius returned?

Why does Darius thank Wayne near the end of this chapter?

ESSAY

This chapter is entitled "Teammates." Why does teamwork always beat out individual performances? Why do you think being a good teammate is so important? How is being a good teammate similar to being a good friend? Are you a good friend/teammate? Explain.

Chapter 7: Time Flies

How many assists did Wayne have during his eighth grade season? What award did he win that year?

What did Wayne think about when he felt bad about being short?

Wayne broke his leg during the first game of his senior season. Describe how it happened using your own words.

ESSAY

In this chapter, Wayne's dream is sidetracked by a bad injury. How is he feeling when he is alone in the hospital bed? Describe a time in your life when something happened and you got sidetracked. (*Hint: This doesn't have to be an injury.) How did you feel? How did you handle the situation?

Chapter 8: A Long Road

Which bone did Wayne break? Why do you think this bone take so long to heal?

When Wayne gets his cast off, is he ready to play hockey again? Explain.

What happened when Wayne finally got back on the ice after his leg had healed?

ESSAY

After reading the first eight chapters of this book, you have gotten to know Wayne pretty well. Describe Wayne's personality. Who does he remind you of? Describe how he is similar or different to this person. (*Hint: You can compare Wayne to somebody you know, yourself, or even someone on TV.)

Chapter 9: Comeback

What subject did Wayne major in during college? How did his major relate to his personal life?

Every day Wayne hops off his bike and walks it up and down the steep hill near his dormitory. Why does he do this? What is he afraid of?

Why do you think Jeff told Wayne about his eighth grade spelling bee?

ESSAY

What does the word perseverance mean? (*Hint: Use a dictionary if you need to.) Does Wayne show this quality when he decides to chase his dream again? Explain. Have you ever persevered through something difficult? Explain.

Chapter 10: Hockey Dreams

Who is Pete Mitchum?

How does Wayne feel about being called Little Wayne at this point in the book?

Which professional team drafted Wayne? Which round was he drafted in?

ESSAY

By the end of *Hockey Dreams*, Wayne has made his dream come true. He chased it down with everything he had. It wasn't easy, but it was worth it! If a book were written about you and your dreams, what would the title be? Describe this book, focusing on the beginning, the middle, and the end.